FURTHERMOOR

DARREN SIMPSON

First published in the UK in 2022 by Usborne Publishing Ltd., Usborne House, 83-85 Saffron Hill, London EC1N 8RT, England. usborne.com
Usborne Verlag, Usborne Publishing Ltd., Prüfeninger Str. 20, 93049 Regensburg, Deutschland, VK Nr. 17560

A CIP catalogue record for this book is available from the British Library.

ISBN 9781474976701 05775 FMAMJJASOND/22

Printed and bound in Great Britain by CPI Group (UK) Ltd, Croydon, CR0 4YY.

PART ONE
WEDNESDAY

For the wallflowers, and for those who refuse to look the other way.

Chapter One

Fifty-nine Bradbury Avenue

When the truth hit Bren, it was as cold and hard as the frost on the window: if he didn't get out of here, he'd die.

It was plain fact. A message to the gut, sent from Bren's tingling toes and hands. His fingers stung as if being pricked by pins of ice, so he hugged himself and shoved his hands beneath his armpits, trying to stop the shivering. But the harder he squeezed himself, the more he shook.

He'd left school about an hour ago; there was still some daylight outside. But not for long. The February sun was sinking. Its pale light oozed through the metal grate covering the window, barely filling this empty, derelict room.

But there was light enough to see. Bren pivoted on the worn carpet, checking for anything he might have missed, anything that might get him out.

There was the stained mattress, propped against the

wall. A radiator, with magnolia paint peeling from its metal. The grated window, looking down upon Bradbury Avenue. And Bren's school backpack, sitting on the floor.

But that was all. There was nothing here that could smash through the window. Nothing to get him through the locked door or even dent its wood.

Bren returned to the window to pound again with his fists – to rap with his knuckles until they bled. He shouted at the glass, crying out for help, though his throat was already raw from yelling.

It was pointless. Even if his voice carried through the double-glazing, no one would hear. No one lived on Bradbury Avenue. It was no man's land. Every terraced house on it was the same. Boarded windows and bricked-up doors. Back gardens full of weeds and litter, nettles and junk.

Bren gave up. His fists left prints on the window, blotching its whorls of spiralling ice. Frost glossed the walls too. The dated floral wallpaper – speckled in places by mould – twinkled in the cold, bluish light.

Bren's woolly gloves were on the floor; he'd taken them off to heave at the door and thump the window. Still shivering, Bren put them back on. He knew the door was jammed, but he tried it again. He rattled and strained at its handle, pulling and pleading as if the door could hear him, then started kicking with his feet. But the door was too thick. It wouldn't budge from its frame.

Grunting hoarsely, Bren grabbed his backpack, pulled the mattress to the floor and sat down. He could feel the cold dampness seeping through his school trousers. When his stomach rumbled, he checked his backpack for something to eat, knowing as he rummaged that there was nothing to find. The food his dad had packed for him that morning was gone – he'd eaten it in the music room at lunchtime.

The thought of Dad made Bren's eyes well up. He'd be worried. Again.

Bren pulled his phone from his duffel coat, looked miserably at its blank screen. He tried turning it on, knowing full well it was dead. There was no way to call anyone. He was trapped.

But then again, maybe not.

Removing a glove again, Bren reached into his trouser pocket and pulled out a watch. The room's silence amplified its steady ticking. It sounded like a knife on a chopping board, hacking the moments into seconds.

Squinting in the gloom, Bren studied the watch. Its olive-green face – set within a simple golden bezel – matched its green strap. There was a round gap at the face's centre, which exposed the cogs working beneath the dial.

Bren watched those golden, ticking hands. Nearly five o'clock.

He curled up on the mattress, put his ear to the watch and closed his eyes.

The ticking went on, lulling him softly. He could feel every tick, every tock, passing through his fingers, travelling up his arms, calming his heart.

Tick.

Tock.

Tick.

Tock.

And then he heard it. A muffled clacking. He opened his eyes.

A section of carpet tightened, before splitting with a soft tearing sound. It parted to reveal golden cogs spinning underneath. They were arranged in a broad ring, with each cog pulling carpet threads to make the tear even wider.

A circle of wooden flooring lay exposed between the cogs. It opened up, like the sliding shutter of a camera lens.

Bright light and birdsong filled the room.

The birdsong of Furthermoor.

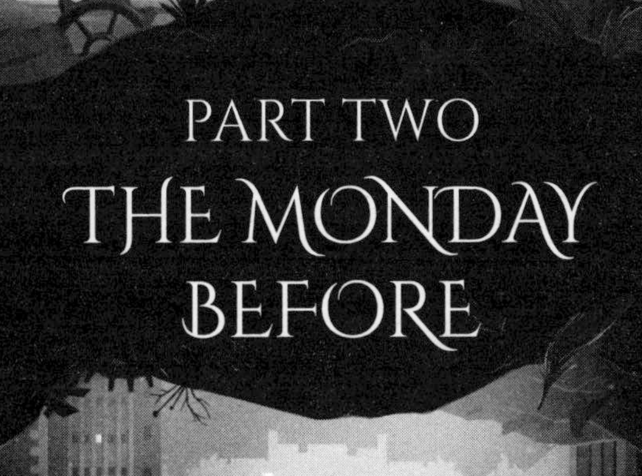

PART TWO
THE MONDAY BEFORE

Chapter Two

Cary

The trouble started with Cary.

Mrs Sendak, head teacher at Williamsborough Academy, had introduced Cary Yue the previous Monday. It was during Mr Okorafor's Year Eight English class. Every eye in the room was on the new boy, but Cary – stood cheerily at the classroom door beside Mrs Sendak – didn't shrink away. Not like new pupils usually do.

"Welcome to Williamsborough Academy, Cary," said Mrs Sendak, smiling mildly. "We had a British-Chinese pupil finish here last year, and she did very well indeed. I'm sure you'll do our school proud."

Cary arched an eyebrow beneath his red-dyed fringe, then rolled his eyes in a way Mrs Sendak couldn't see, which prompted sniggers from some of the students.

Bren watched Cary stroll towards an empty seat by the whiteboard. Though he was short – and perhaps a tad on the plump side – Cary walked at full height, with his back straight, happily meeting the gaze of every student. He didn't seem fazed at all by the whispers and giggles from the back of the class.

Bren glanced about the room, watching the other students. He saw Shaun tilting his close-cropped head, tracking Cary as he crossed the room. Shaun's blue eyes were narrow and cold.

Bren knew that look. Shaun was measuring up new prey.

Shaun glanced suddenly at Bren, as if he'd sensed him watching. His lips curled into a sneer. Bren looked away.

He should have been more careful. Should have kept his head down.

After Cary got settled at his desk, Mr Okorafor prompted a chorus of groans by setting a speed essay on George Orwell's *Animal Farm*. Hence the loud cheers when the bell finally rang for lunch.

Pupils barrelled by while Mr Okorafor gathered up essays. Bren kept his eyes on his books as he packed them away, and waited for the worst of the rush to pass before skulking to the door.

The corridor outside was busier than he'd expected. Caught by surprise, Bren lowered his head and veered away from the crowd that – rather than making for the school cafeteria – had gathered a few steps from English class.

As keen as Bren was to get to the music room, curiosity

got the better of him. Hugging himself into the smallest possible shape, he stopped by a wall display about *Macbeth* and lingered discreetly, keeping his distance from everyone else.

Giggles and laughter erupted, and Bren saw Cary at the centre of the crowd, grinning and gesturing busily with his hands.

Cary flicked his red fringe from his eyes. He said something that must have been even funnier, because everyone started really cracking up.

Everyone, that is, apart from Shaun.

Like Bren, Shaun hovered at the edge of the throng, looking in from the outside. Bren didn't want to repeat the mistake of meeting Shaun's eyes, so he did his best to watch him sidelong, with his head still tilted low. He could see that Shaun wasn't impressed. Every laugh from Cary's audience made Shaun's long forehead crease further, and his black eyebrows met above his nose, sinking in disapproval.

Shaun must have had enough. He pushed a nearby pupil aside, and when others saw him coming they moved quickly out of his path.

Cary watched cheerfully while Shaun closed in. Shaun moved with his usual slow swagger. His eyes were locked firmly on his prey.

"You alright?" asked Cary.

Shaun drew up to him at full height. He stepped closer, so that his toes were almost touching Cary's, and looked down from above, leering smugly, waiting for Cary to cringe or back into the wall.

But Cary didn't move. He just met Shaun's gaze, his smile unwavering. "You're a bit close, bud. Mind stepping back? My nose is like, *this close* to your armpit, and I'm guessing you're out of deodorant."

Bren couldn't believe his ears. A smatter of nervous giggles rippled through the corridor, only to be silenced when Shaun looked around to see who was laughing. The group took a collective step back. Bren pressed himself against the wall.

Cary seemed puzzled, but only for a moment. He peered up again, straight into Shaun's face. "Oh right. I get it." His eyes narrowed and his smile was back. "You're the alpha male around here, right? And this is you banging your chest, reminding everyone who's boss. Is that right?"

Shaun's pale cheeks reddened and he drew back, just a little. He scratched the black stubble of his hair, then glanced fiercely about to find an audience still hovering.

After pressing his knuckles into his palm, he cocked his head at Cary, then reached out and flicked his fringe. "What's this rubbish in your hair? You trying to turn yourself into a ginge?"

"It's red," replied Cary. "There's a difference. What's your problem? You don't like it?"

Shaun shook his head, his sneer returning. "It looks stupid."

"You honestly think I give the slightest about what you think of my hair? Don't flatter yourself, bud."

Gasps and whispers. Bren watched the other students. They were as gripped as he was.

Shaun's nostrils flared. He stepped close again, looming over Cary. But again, Cary refused to give an inch.

"You'd better watch that mouth," rumbled Shaun. "Big words for a little man. Shouldn't you be cooking noodles with your mum and dad at a takeaway or something?"

Cary screwed up his face. "Great. Racism. Didn't take long, did it?" He sighed and shook his head. "Is that all you've got? Stereotypes older than my nan?"

Shaun was breathing heavily. His eyes – usually a cold, bright blue – were dark and thin.

"FYI, my parents don't run a takeaway," Cary went on. "My mum's an engineer and my dad does photography. Not that there's anything wrong with working in a takeaway. You want me to assume some stuff about you?" He looked Shaun up and down, then stood on his toes to sniff the air by Shaun's chin.

Cary screwed up his face as Shaun pulled away. "Alright then. Going by your breath, I'm guessing you haven't seen a toothbrush in years." He wafted a hand. "Honest, bud – you could knock out a pony."

He must have clocked Shaun's clenching fists. "And that's next, is it? You're gonna get physical, cos you've got nothing left up here?" He tapped his own forehead.

"*You little—*"

"I'm hungry." Cary was already brushing past him. "Got better things to do. See you around, yeah?"

Caught off guard, Shaun blinked and turned to see Cary heading for the cafeteria. The crowd began to scatter and follow, tittering in low tones while being careful not to glance in Shaun's direction.

Bren had been preoccupied picking his jaw up from the floor. He began to move away but the delay cost him. He'd only managed a few steps along the corridor when Shaun called for him.

"*Hey*. Ginger nut."

Bren froze.

"Come here."

Bren's eyes darted around the corridor. It was empty. Everyone was gone.

"I said *come here*, beakface."

Bren hated being called beakface – even more so than ginger nut. His nose had a pronounced bridge – something he'd inherited from his dad – but it was hardly big.

Sighing, and with his eyes to the floor, Bren turned and

shuffled towards Shaun. There was no point trying to run. That only ever made things worse.

"Where're your manners?" grunted Shaun. "You should look up when your betters are talking to you."

Bren raised his gaze. Shaun still looked a bit thrown by what had happened with Cary; he was scratching the back of his head, and his thin lips were tight at their edges. But when Bren did as he was told and drew reluctantly closer, Shaun's mouth tugged itself into a sly, lopsided smile.

He watched Bren squirm for some moments, before nodding to himself, satisfied. "Did you think that was funny?"

Bren swallowed. "What?"

"The new boy: fake-ginge. That stuff he said. Did you find it funny?"

Bren's hand stroked the green watch in his pocket. He wanted so badly to be away from here – to be in the music room, safe and alone.

He shook his head.

"Good. Cos it was lame." Shaun sucked in his lips, snorted through his nose. "New boy's a loser. Just like you, ginger nut." He gave Bren a small shove. "What are you?"

Bren's gaze was on the floor once more. "Loser," he croaked.

"Louder."

"*I'm a loser.*"

"That's right. At least *you* know your place. Cary'll know his too, when I'm done with him." Shaun nodded to himself again, before cracking his knuckles. "You know, I haven't seen you around lately. You been hiding from me?"

Bren shook his head.

Shaun stuck out his lower lip and put on a babyish, mollycoddling voice. "I've missed you. Have you missed me?"

Bren couldn't speak. His mouth was too dry.

"Haven't you?" Shaun's blue eyes became slits.

Bren nodded.

"So say it."

Bren's words were hoarse. "I missed you."

"Good." With a flash of his arm, Shaun shoved Bren again, harder this time. Staggering backwards, Bren glanced up to see Shaun stepping towards him, his lips peeling back to reveal gritted teeth. "So let's catch up, yeah? It's—"

He was silenced by the creak of a door.

When Mr Okorafor stepped out from the classroom, he found Shaun lingering casually in the corridor with his hands in his pockets. Bren tried to look casual too, biting his lip and staring at the scuffs on his shoes.

"Everything okay, boys?"

"Sure, Mr Okorafor," replied Shaun.

"And you, Bren?"

Bren raised his eyes. Mr Okorafor was smiling gently at him, though his dark forehead was wrinkled beneath his greying curls. Bren glanced discreetly at Shaun – who glowered at him, just for a moment – and did his best to return the English teacher's smile. "Good, thanks."

Mr Okorafor gave a slow nod. "Okay. Well… Shouldn't you both be having your lunch?"

Shaun pointed down the corridor. "Going there now. Starvin'."

Bren was already scuttling the other way, bound for the coat in his locker.

Chapter Three
The Tunnel Tree

Bren hunched up his shoulders, skulking along the fence that separated the playground from the main road. The cold air was alive with noise: calls from the students playing football, the scuff and clop of school shoes against concrete, catcalls and laughter, natter and babble.

He had his hands in his duffel coat and could see his breath leaving him in clouds. The caretaker had scattered grit and salt on the playground that morning, but a thick frost still lingered at its edges.

Bren peered furtively at the football match while he passed. The ball was followed by whoops and cries as it shot between two backpack goalposts. When the scoring champion ran a lap round the makeshift pitch, Bren tried to remember how it felt to sprint like that with everyone watching – with your arms in the air and cheers in your ears. It seemed unimaginable now.

Bren stared at his feet and kept walking. He paused before hitting the path from the main building to the arts block, then turned to check the playground in case Shaun, Isaiah or Alex were watching. The last thing Bren wanted was Shaun and his lackeys figuring out where he went every lunch break.

They didn't seem to be about, so Bren continued on his way, passing the trees that lined the path and pushing through a glass door.

The arts block was always deserted during lunchtime. That was why Bren liked it. He opened his backpack and began wolfing down lunch, all the while hurrying past wall displays plastered with pop art. Then he eased a door open and – after checking no one was around – entered the school's music room.

The space was shabby and cramped, with metal chairs folded along one wall, and instruments piled in cases along the other. After finishing a banana and shoving its peel into the lunch box in his bag, Bren crossed the room and sat on the carpet in the far corner, safely out of sight behind a battered drum kit.

He'd already pulled the watch from his pocket. He brushed his thumb across its green face, then closed his eyes and held it against his ear, allowing his heartbeat to settle into the clock's ticking rhythm. His stiff shoulders sank, losing their tautness.

Tick.

Tock.

Tick.

Tock.

The rumble of a drum skin had him opening his eyes. With a smile dawning on his face, Bren watched the drums revolve and shift. They clicked and clattered as they rolled, until the drum kit rearranged itself with its biggest drum facing upwards.

Pocketing his watch, Bren got up to see the drum skin roll away like a window blind, then peered through its opening at the hole in the floor. He saw Furthermoor's canopy glittering far below – the tops of trees with leaves of green crystal. A tree directly below began to move, corkscrewing upwards towards Bren's hole in the sky.

The treetop stopped turning when its tip entered the drum. Bren clambered on and climbed a little way down the tree, passing cables and pulleys embedded in its smooth wooden trunk. Then he sat cheerfully on a branch, with his legs dangling in warm, sun-filled light.

Taking the watch out once more, Bren opened its face to reveal an interior packed with cogs. He skimmed and twirled them with his fingers, hitting a sequence that made the tree – with pulleys twisting in the grooves of its wood – turn and lower itself back towards the ground.

Bren sank through the canopy of crystal leaves. He saw

the forest floor dappled by sun and – as soon as he was close enough – dropped from the branch to the ground.

With the tree grinding to a halt behind him, Bren smiled and took in a long, deep breath. The air smelt of sandalwood, bronze and polish. He rocked a little on his heels, enjoying the green wool and woodchip underfoot. A breeze ruffled the trees, causing emerald leaves to twinkle and chime. Bren tweaked the watch's cogs, this time striking the combination that controlled the wind. He adjusted the breeze, turning it up and down so that the musical chiming grew louder, then softer.

When he'd found the right volume for his mood, he sauntered through the woods. His playground stoop fell away with every step, and he was soon walking tall between the trees. He called out.

"Evie?"

A restrained shout came in reply, from somewhere nearby. "*Over here.*"

Bren heard a tiny whirring by his ear, and a nickel dragonfly darted back and forth not far from his nose. He wanted a better look at its delicate, stained-glass wings, so he adjusted the watch again. Pulleys in the grooves that criss-crossed the ground began to churn, tightening cables and tugging gears in the trees. With a deep creaking groan, the emerald canopy above Bren shifted. A clockwork robin with a breast of red cotton soared from a branch. As more sun poured into the woods, its light hit the dragonfly with a burst of shimmering colour.

Bren beamed at the dragonfly's wings and jewelled eyes, before calling out again. "Over where?"

"*By the tunnel tree.*"

While Bren strolled, crystal ferns shook with the scurrying of unseen creatures. He entered a small glade and saw Evie at its far edge. She was sitting by an immense tree that straddled a hillock of wool-moss, with its roots clinging like fingers to steep fuzzy slopes. Trails of emerald ivy – as bright and brittle as the finest glass – tumbled around the mound, and the tree's thick roots framed a dark, burrow-like opening into the ground.

"Hey, big sis," said Bren.

"Sshh," hissed Evie, keeping as still as she could. Her gaze was set on her freckled arm, which was stretched out and still, and host to a row of mechanized butterflies.

The glade's light made her hair shine like copper. She had the same unruly locks as Bren, though their red tangles flowed down to her waist. Evie also had the same hazel eyes and slightly beakish nose, but unlike Bren she wore glasses, with olive frames that stood out against her pale skin.

Bren mirrored Evie's pose, sitting beside her with his legs crossed. She was a couple of years older than him, and sat taller in her floral summer dress, with less of Bren's gangliness.

Evie didn't even glance at him. The butterflies on her arm had golden abdomens and wings of patterned silk. Bren laughed when a few of them twitched their wings. "You know I can make them stay put, right?" He held up the green watch.

"Of course I know," whispered Evie. "But I want to do this myself."

"Suit yourself."

Evie kept her hazel eyes on the butterflies. "So, how's real life?"

Bren peered back the way he'd come, thinking of the hole in the sky he'd just climbed through. "Not as nice as here." He rested a palm on one of the tunnel tree's roots.

"Uh oh. Have the teachers been lecturing you again about daydreaming in class?"

"Not today."

"Then what's happened?"

"Shaun." Bren let out a sigh. "Shaun's happened."

A ginger eyebrow rose behind Evie's glasses. "I thought you were staying off his radar?"

"I was. But I messed up, dropped my guard. Plus, there's a new boy at school."

Evie lowered her arm, sending a cloud of clockwork butterflies into the air. "Oh yeah? What's he like?"

"Cocky." Bren opened the watch and turned some tiny silver wheels, conjuring an image that shimmered above the cogs: Cary at the classroom door with Mrs Sendak, beaming back at the gawping class.

"Draws way too much attention to himself," continued Bren, shaking the image away.

"Not everyone's as allergic to the limelight as you, Bren. There's no harm in enjoying a bit of attention now and then." Evie scratched her nose. "Don't you think?"

Bren didn't answer. He was watching a beetle climb a porcelain toadstool. Its copper shell shone golden-green, before parting to reveal thin glass wings. Bren could see the tiny gears beneath them; they whirred as the beetle launched itself and buzzed clumsily through the air.

Evie's voice rose a little. "Don't ignore me, Bren. It's one thing ignoring the real world, but another to ignore your older sister."

Bren chuckled and turned his gaze to her. "Sometimes you sound just like Mum. Blah blah blah, do-this-do-that."

"How is Mum?"

"The usual. Always busy, working late. And when she's not busy she's nagging at me to get out more, see some friends."

"Maybe she's got a point."

Bren shifted the subject. "You fancy heading to the lake?" He got up and brushed woodchip from his trousers.

"How much time do we have?"

A shrug from Bren. "Dunno." Time in Furthermoor

rarely tallied with the real world; it was always hard to tell how much had really passed. "Hopefully enough. It's lunch break."

"Okay. It'll be nice to stretch my legs."

Bren gave the tunnel tree an affectionate pat before they left the glade. They were soon following a blue crystal stream, as frozen in its frothing as a brook in a photograph. After a while the trees fell away, and the stream met a sapphire lake hemmed by silk reeds.

The pair stepped onto the lake's hard blue surface. Evie was barefoot, as usual. She never wore shoes in Furthermoor.

Taking her cue, Bren removed his shoes and socks and carried them while he walked, enjoying the sun-warmed sapphire on his soles. Shadowy shapes moved beneath the surface. Huge fish with motorized, sweeping tails. Clockwork otters, gliding to and fro.

Reaching the centre of the lake, Bren dropped his shoes and opened the watch. When he flicked the teeth of several cogs, two sections of sapphire rose by his feet, before flipping slowly to reveal deckchairs attached to their undersides.

"Nice," said Evie, easing herself onto the stripy canvas. Bren flopped into the other chair.

He was happy to sit in silence, savouring Furthermoor's tranquillity – its safety and simplicity. A shrill, croak-like warble broke the lull, and Bren looked up to see a mechanical heron soaring through the sky. Sunlight caught the silk of its billowing wings.

Evie stirred on her chair. "So, what happened with Shaun? You said it's something to do with that new boy?"

Bren groaned. "Cary. He's got a death wish. Shaun squared up to him in the corridor after English. Showing him who's boss or whatever. But Cary wasn't having it."

"There was a fight?"

"No. If there was, Cary'd be dead. He's half the size of Shaun. But he just...sort of..." Bren shook his head, frowning now. "I don't know *what* he did. He just...wasn't scared. He stood his ground, even though Shaun could have squashed him with his thumb. And more than that – Cary actually made *fun* of Shaun. Told him his breath could knock out a pony."

"*What?*" Evie broke into a snicker. Bren felt his frown fading. Evie's laugh always did that.

Bren went on. "He made Shaun look like...a loser. In front of everyone."

"Wow. Sounds awesome."

Bren scratched his freckled nose. "It was...cool, I guess. But Shaun was peeved. And who do you think he took it out on?"

Evie's smile fell away. "Oh." She leaned forward then, to put a hand on Bren's knee. "What did he do?"

"A couple of shoves. Mr Okorafor turned up before things got worse."

"Close call."

"It's not over though, Evie. Mr Okorafor isn't always going to be around, and Shaun won't be done with me yet. You know what he's like. He never forgets." Bren chewed nervously at his thumb. "Cary's got no idea what he's let himself in for."

Evie nodded slowly to herself. "Well. Maybe he…knows what he's doing?"

"If he knew what he was doing he'd have kept his head down."

"Hm." Evie pushed her lips out slightly, the way she always did when she was concentrating. "Well, at least he's standing up for himself. Not everyone's got the guts to do that."

Bren glowered at his sister. "What's that supposed to mean?"

"Nothing." Evie looked away and slid down in her chair, crossing her ankles with one of her heels on the lake's hard surface. She let her head loll towards the sky. "Just saying, that's all."

"There's a difference between being brave and being stupid, you know."

Evie shrugged. "I guess."

Bren straightened in his seat. "Shouldn't you be on my side?"

"Why's that?"

"You're my sister."

Evie scrunched her face. "So?"

Bren eyed her for some moments, until a smile crept onto his lips. He jiggled the watch at her. "You're lucky I can't control you with this."

Evie smirked. "You always say that, but you're bluffing. You like me to be myself." She tilted her head. "Or would you prefer me to be like one of your –" her eyes followed another heron that was crossing the sky – "gorgeous machines?"

Bren grinned and wriggled his eyebrows, still dangling the watch. "I'd make your hair fall out."

"Big deal. Hair's overrated."

"I'd give you long yellow fingernails."

"All the better for scratching my back."

"I'd give you lumpy wooden legs."

Evie laughed. "I'd use them to kick your butt!"

Bren laughed back. "Oh yeah? Well how about—" He stopped, startled by a faint, far-away ringing. He cocked his ear. "School bell."

"Oh dear," said Evie, still smirking. "You'd better get to your next lesson. You've got work to do." She stretched out lazily on the chair, with her hands behind her head.

"Try not to rub it in, yeah?"

The pair of them exchanged smiles and – after putting his socks and shoes on – Bren began to run across the lake.

Evie called out after him. "You visiting tonight?"

"Course I am!"

The watch was already in Bren's palm, with its face open and interior exposed. He eyed a tree mottled by jade lichen at the lake's edge, and adjusted some cogs to make it revolve in the ground.

Bren climbed the tree while it corkscrewed and rose, and was soon clambering through a drum to take up his position against the music room's wall. With the watch once again against his ear, he counted the seconds and waited.

Tock.

Tick.

Tock.

Tick.

Chapter Four
Someone Like You

Bren dashed across the playground and through the school entrance. Staying back from any crowds, he lowered his face and skulked through the corridors. Other pupils bustled around him, bound for their lessons.

When a hand touched his shoulder, he spun and almost yelped, but was relieved to see it was just his English teacher.

"Mr Okorafor…"

"Hello, Bren. Sorry to stop you. I just wanted a quick word about your *Animal Farm* essay from earlier. Or rather…the lack of it."

"Um." Bren gave his neck an awkward rub. He'd been gazing out of the window, lost in his thoughts, while everyone else was getting on with their essays. "Sorry, Mr Okorafor."

"You barely made it past the introduction."

"I... I'm really sorry. I meant to write it. I just got...um..."

"Distracted." Mr Okorafor shook his head and sighed. "This isn't the first time this has happened, Bren. You wasted a lesson last week by staring into space. And I heard in the staffroom that you're drifting off in other lessons too. Frankly, I'm a little concerned."

Bren lowered his eyes.

"You've become quite the daydreamer," continued Mr Okorafor. He stroked his thin grey beard with his finger and thumb, before clearing his throat uneasily. "Now, I realize things can't be easy after...what happened last year. That's perfectly understandable. But if this continues to be a regular habit, it'll impact your academic progress. And I'd hate to see that. You're a really bright boy."

Bren stared at his hands. "Thank you, Mr Okorafor."

"And you know we have people you can talk to, Bren. People who can help with...however you might be feeling."

Though Bren lifted his face to his teacher, he couldn't look him in the eye. "No. No need. I'm fine."

Mr Okorafor watched him for several seconds, before nodding gently. "Okay. If you're sure. But you really need to up your game. If things go on this way, I'll have no choice but to mention it to Mrs Sendak. She might want to talk to your parents."

"There's no need!" blurted Bren. "I'll focus more, I promise. It won't happen again."

Mr Okorafor scratched one of his dark cheeks, then gave a tired shrug. "Finish that essay tonight and bring it to me first thing in the morning. 'Power tends to corrupt and absolute power corrupts absolutely.' I need you to write about how that quote relates to *Animal Farm*. Okay? If you do a good job, I won't speak to Mrs Sendak. Deal?"

"Deal. Thanks, Mr Okorafor."

Before his teacher had even turned away, Bren was scuttling through corridors again. But as he took a corner he glanced up and froze.

Shaun. Leaning against some lockers. Chatting to Alex and Isaiah, obviously in no rush to get to class.

Praying he hadn't been seen, Bren turned quietly, aiming to hide round the corner until Shaun disappeared. But before he could even take a step, he heard Shaun holler.

"Beakface! Where d' you think *you're* going?"

Bren froze again.

"I'm talking to you, ginge. Turn around and come here."

With his head sinking deeper between his shoulders, Bren turned around.

A few other students were still rushing through the corridor. After pausing to assess the scene, they looked sheepishly away and made more hastily for their classrooms.

Another ring of the bell. Lessons were starting.

Bren looked up and down the empty corridor. His gaze

drifted wretchedly to Shaun, Isaiah and Alex. Isaiah, with his short black dreads and fuzzy moustache, was as tall as Shaun. The pair of them looked like they belonged in the next year up. Alex was the shortest of the three, but made up for it with muscle. The top buttons of his school shirt were undone, showing off the thick trunk of his neck.

Smirking now, Shaun peeled away from the lockers. He beckoned with a finger.

Bren's gaze went to the floor. He dragged himself reluctantly forward.

"We've got unfinished business," jeered Shaun.

When Bren was close enough, Shaun used his knuckle to lift Bren's chin. Bren had no choice but to look up. He saw Shaun's head tilting to one side. His eyes were bright with glee, shining ice-blue against that pale, hard face. Alex and Isaiah were stood either side of him, grinning and waiting like well-trained hunting dogs.

Moving suddenly, Shaun grabbed Bren's shoulders and – with a hard thump – pinned his back against the lockers. "So where were we, loser?"

The more Bren cringed, the more Shaun grinned. There was a keen, feral hunger in his eyes. He jerked his head playfully to and fro, and Bren flinched every time. Alex and Isaiah chortled at each wince, until their grunts were silenced by another voice in the corridor.

"Oh my god. Are you seriously at it again?"

It was Cary, strolling towards them with disgust written all over his brow.

Shaun's smile twisted itself into a scowl. He released Bren and turned to Cary, who'd stopped just a couple of metres away.

Cary frowned and angled his head, considering Shaun, Alex and Isaiah as if they were specimens in a lab. "I mean, what's your problem? I'm properly curious."

Shaun didn't reply. Alex and Isaiah glanced sidelong at him. Their expressions were conflicted – hawkish but puzzled.

Cary peered past the three of them towards Bren. His features softened and he beckoned with a friendly hand. "You wanna come away from that locker?"

Bren's eyes went to Shaun, whose finger flew out towards him, ordering him to stay.

Shaun tipped his head back to look down his nose at Cary. "You can't tell him what to do."

Cary scoffed. "And you can?" He spoke to Bren. "Come on, bud. You don't have to do as he says."

Bren's pupils flitted back and forth between Shaun and Cary. He swallowed uncomfortably and – after giving Cary a dismal, apologetic look – stayed put against the lockers, as if still held there in Shaun's grip.

Shaun flashed him a wolfish smile. "Good boy." He turned back to Cary, smug in his victory. "So much for the knight in shining armour. What're you playing at anyway? Is this like...gingers together or something?" He snorted a laugh and nudged Alex and Isaiah. The pair cackled, though not without a second's delay. To Bren, Isaiah and Alex still seemed perplexed by Cary. Wary, even.

Cary pointed at his dyed fringe. "I've already told you: it's red, not ginger. What are you? Stupid or colour-blind?"

Shaun's jaw became rigid. His chest rose and he seemed to get taller, with both hands balling into big, bony fists. When he stepped towards Cary, Isaiah and Alex moved with him. They looked more confident now, back in familiar territory.

But again, Cary didn't give an inch. He looked at Shaun's rising fists with genuine loathing. "Great. So we're back here again. You can't think of anything to say, so you're going to let your fists do the talking."

"Maybe that way you'll listen."

The trio took another step forward, towering over Cary. But Cary refused to cower.

"So what happens now?" he asked. "You three pile onto me? To show how hard you are?" Cary rolled his eyes. "Reeeeal tough, picking a fight with someone when they're outnumbered three to one." He tutted. "Even if you kick me in, I think I'll know who the real losers are in *that* fight."

Shaun faltered, then used his palms to steer Alex and Isaiah away, so that only he and Cary were toe to toe. While the pair of them grimaced at each other, the silence stretched out, taut and unbearable.

"*Boo!*" crowed Shaun, jabbing suddenly with his fist. He stopped just short of hitting Cary's stomach, but it was close enough to make Cary flinch.

Though the flinch was gone in an instant, Shaun saw it and his grimace became a grin.

Cary held Shaun's gaze, his expression hard once more. But Bren could see how his body had tightened. It trembled faintly, as if bracing for a smack.

Shaun nodded to himself, apparently satisfied. "You know what, Cary? I think we're gonna have fun getting to know each other. I've got geography now, but let's catch up some other time, yeah?"

Shaun winked at Cary before turning to Bren, who was still pressed against the lockers. "You and me'll catch up too, beakface." He hit Alex and Isaiah's arms with the backs of his fingers. "Come on. Let's leave these losers alone."

His arm barged into Cary's as he passed, prompting the usual sniggers from Isaiah and Alex.

Bren stayed put until they turned the corner. The second they were out of sight, he let out the breath he'd been holding in his lungs, slumping slightly as he left the lockers. Then he looked up, grimacing at Cary, his tone sarcastic. "Thanks a bunch."

Cary looked confused. "You're...welcome?"

"You should have left us alone. I had things under control."

"You did?" Cary didn't sound convinced.

Bren shook his head. "You don't get it. If you just give in to them, they get bored in the end and leave you alone. But now you've wound up Shaun, and he's gonna go on a mission to make my life hell."

Cary's eyebrows sank. "So he's given you hassle before?"

Bren couldn't help glancing away. He crossed his arms.

Cary stepped forward, studying Bren closely with his brown eyes. "Man, I'm sorry you guys have got history. But you know the deal, right? If you keep letting him push you around, he'll never stop. I bet he came for you cos I dissed him after English. Probably trying to big himself up again."

"Great. Well, thanks for sending him my way."

Cary frowned. "Sorry. If I'd known he had…someone like you…"

Bren's head jerked up. His arms stiffened by his sides. "What do you mean, 'someone like me'?"

Cary bit his lower lip. A faint blush coloured his cheeks. "That came out wrong." He cleared his throat. "Hey, what's your name?"

"Bren."

"You wanna hang out some time? Maybe I can help you. You know, with Shaun."

"You've done enough, thanks."

"But—"

"What's it got to do with you, anyway? Why don't you just mind your own business?"

"What, like everyone else?" Cary peered about the corridor. "Like all the others who turn a blind eye when Shaun pushes you around?" He watched Bren closely. "I bet most of them do, right?"

Bren's mouth flapped open and shut. He shoved his hands into his pockets. "They're just looking out for themselves."

"Yeah. Looking out for themselves." A snort from Cary. "Look. I've been in your shoes. Been the only Chinese kid in a few schools. I know what it's like to be singled out and given a hard time. And I know how most people look the other way. It's not a great feeling, is it?"

Bren didn't answer.

Cary shook his head. "I'm not gonna be one of those people. No way, bud."

"I'm late for my lesson." Bren started walking, passing Cary with his eyes fixed ahead.

"Lessons, yeah – about that," began Cary. "Do you know where I can find room B Seven?"

Bren wanted to keep walking. He wanted to get away as quickly as possible, before Cary stirred up more trouble or started lecturing again. But he found himself slowing down to reply. "Just keep going the way you're heading. It's on the left."

"Thanks."

Bren slowed a little more, then stopped and turned to face Cary. "Listen. Shaun's *really* going to have it in for you now. He never forgets. If you want my advice, steer clear of the bike shelter at break times. That's where Shaun usually hangs out. Stay close to the playground edge. They're less likely to notice you there. And listen out before you go into the toilets, in case Shaun's in there. Being caught in the bogs never ends well. And if Shaun's at the school gate when you're coming in or out, you can use the car park's gate instead."

Cary cocked his head. "Is that everything?"

"No. If Shaun gets hold of you and...you know...hurts you or whatever, don't grass him up to anyone, or he'll just make things *way* worse for you. Okay?"

Cary didn't respond.

Bren frowned, trying to read his expression. "Okay?" he repeated.

Cary sighed. "Bren. I don't think that's the best way to handle Shaun. You can't keep being..." He trailed off.

Bren's eyes narrowed. "Being what?"

Cary nodded towards the locker Shaun had pinned Bren against. "Like that. Just taking it from him."

"You think I have a choice?"

"Well...yeah." Cary gave an awkward shrug. "I guess so."

Bren spluttered. "You *guess* so?" He rubbed angrily at his

hair, making it messier than it already was. "You… You don't know *anything* about me! You don't know anything about…about this school!"

"Maybe not. But I know a thing or two about bullies."

"Yeah?" huffed Bren. "Well, me too." He turned and continued to class.

Chapter Five

No Good Deed

The school bell rang for the final time that day. Before its chime had even faded, pupils were shooting up from their desks and shoving books into bags.

Moving slowly, Bren left his class and joined the torrent of students. The corridors rang out with shouts and banter. Bren fetched his duffel coat from his locker and – staying always by the walls – followed other students to the exit. Laughs and cackles made him raise his eyes, and he saw Cary just ahead, giggling with Year Eight's most popular girls.

Cary must have sensed him watching. His head turned and he gave Bren a friendly wave, before beckoning him to join the crowd. Shaking his head, Bren hugged himself and hung back until Cary was out of sight.

February's chill hit him hard when he reached the playground. He fastened his coat's toggles and pulled up his hood, watching through cloudy breaths as students practised skids on the frost. The sun hung low and pale in the sky, seemingly giving off more cold than heat. As Bren followed the path from the playground he clocked Shaun ahead, guffawing with Alex and Isaiah by the gate. Stooping low behind some other pupils, Bren passed the gate unseen and left through the car park.

He was soon heading down Williamsborough Dale, the main road that ran through the estate. Trundling cars – many of them old, some scarred by long scratches – moved along the icy road, beeping at drivers who'd stopped for too long while their kids hopped in.

Red-brick houses lined both sides of the road, parting only for the potholed, terraced streets that broke off regularly left and right. A few homes were covered in pebble-dash, which crumbled here and there to expose weathered bricks beneath.

Bren glanced about the Dale, taking in the betting shop with its usual circle of smokers, all huddled up and puffing by the door; the chippy with its delicious oily smell; the bus stops with their cracked glass panes; the local pub – the Gladstone – and kebab shop.

Pupils from the academy were pouring into the newsagent's, before coming out again with sweets and fizzy drinks. A couple of older boys stood not far from the door, sucking at cigarettes and squinting through the smoke.

Something small and dark caught Bren's eye, at the edge of the road not far from his feet. He stooped a little, staring at the bird huddled by the kerb. Its legs and wings were tucked in, and it looked to Bren like a crow, but smaller than the ones he usually saw around Williamsborough. And though its feathers were black, Bren saw hints of brown in those oily-looking plumes.

A car rolled by with its wheels just centimetres away, causing the bird to ruffle and squawk. Its open beak exposed a tiny pink mouth.

When another car rumbled by, Bren mumbled at the bird, willing it to get up and fly to safety. But it wouldn't move.

Perhaps it was injured. Bren glanced up and down the road. The bird would be crushed beneath a wheel if it stayed put.

Grunting, and wishing he'd brought his gloves, he crouched and gathered the bird in his hands. It felt so bony against Bren's fingers, and his heart began to race as it flapped and screeched. When it pecked his finger Bren gasped and let go, staggering back and wincing.

The bird had taken a tumble, but at least it was on the pavement now.

"You're welcome," muttered Bren. He was nursing his finger when he sensed something wrong – like an abrupt change of air pressure, right by his head. There was a heavy flutter, a rasping caw, and something thumped the top of his hood. Bren's eyes followed the flapping sound. He saw a huge crow rising through the air to perch on a tree.

It wasn't alone. Four other crows shared the same branch, glaring blackly at Bren with dark, beady eyes.

And then it happened again, this time from the front: a crow swooped right at him, with its claws raised and aimed at his face. Bren spun and felt something tear into his hood.

"Hey!" His voice broke with panic. "I was trying to help!"

He whirled when another crow sliced through the air, this time clawing the hands he'd raised to protect his face. The pain was savage, and when Bren saw blood he broke into a run.

Bren had no idea where he was fleeing to. He just felt his legs pounding beneath him, the soles of his shoes skidding on frost. The air teemed with caws and thrashing wings. Bren's hands were up and flailing, knocking away those dagger-black beaks. Again: the sharp scratch of talons, the red shock of blood.

Bren ran and ran. His heart was beating so hard he could hear it in his ears. He only began to slow when he realized the flapping had stopped. Panting for breath, he turned back around, with his trembling hands guarding his face.

Not a crow in sight. They'd left him alone.

As his eyes left the trees they moved to quiet terraces, to the tiny off-licence across the road, to Williamsborough Dale at the top of the street.

Bren realized with a groan where he was.

Lewis Road.

And that meant one thing: Ballard Tower.

Pivoting again, Bren saw the apartment block looming before him, just beyond a stretch of frosty grass. Small windows glimmered across its broad side, and Bren could see the exposed concrete corridors that connected the lift tower to the main block.

Bren used to like Ballard Tower. He used to see friends there. Used to play football on that very grass. And while a lot of Williamsborough's locals thought the tower was ugly, Bren thought it was beautiful. He loved its solidity, its simplicity. Its permanence. It looked like the launch tower for a rocket sent to the stars by some ancient civilization. Something left behind that would never crumble away.

A cruel shout rang through the air, reminding Bren of why he no longer came here.

"Ginger nut!"

Bren pushed the heels of his palms into his eyes. As if this day could get any worse.

When he lowered his hands he saw Shaun ahead, taking

a shortcut across the field to the tower, on his way home from school.

Pulling away from some other pupils, Shaun began to head in Bren's direction. Bren took a timid step back.

"Stay!" barked Shaun.

Bren's mouth was dry as ash by the time Shaun reached him. He couldn't even swallow, and found himself hiding his bloodied hands in his pockets.

"Hey, beakface." Leering happily, Shaun put a hand into Bren's hood to pat his cheek. "Haven't seen you round here in a *long* time. Dead keen today, aren't you?"

"I..." Bren didn't know what to say. His mind was still reeling from the crows.

Shaun pushed out his lower lip. "Why so sad, freckle-face? I figured you'd be—"

He was interrupted by sounds of giddy laughter. Bren twisted on the spot, following Shaun's gaze to see three older Year Eight girls coming up Lewis Road. They were chatting and giggling, with their eyes on their phones. As they passed, one of them gave Shaun a wave.

"Hey, Shaun. Becks's parents are out. You wanna come hang at the flat?"

Shaun was beaming. He put an arm round Bren as if they were best buddies. Bren noticed how he'd spread his legs on the frost; how he swept a hand over the stubble on his head, as if there was hair there to tidy.

"Yeah, alright," replied Shaun. Bren could swear he'd lowered the pitch of his voice. "When you heading up?"

The girl pushed her dark bangs out of her eyes. "Like, literally right now. Gotta make the most of it, right?"

"Cool. I'll be up in a bit, yeah?"

Shaun watched the girls from behind as they continued on their way to Ballard Tower. Then he released Bren and leaned close to peer into his hood. His smile tightened into something stiffer, meaner. Bren felt every one of his muscles contracting, ready for a sudden kick or cuff.

But Shaun laughed and gave him a punch on the arm. "You know what? I've had my fill of you today. Much as I like your company, it's not as good as theirs." He tipped his head towards the tower, then gave Bren another pat on the cheek. "So go home, yeah? Like a good boy."

Bren didn't need to be told twice. But as he took a step backwards he heard a jingle from across the road. Shaun's smile fell away, and Bren turned to see Shaun's dad leaving the off-licence.

"Oi! Shaun!" One of Shaun's dad's hands was weighed down by a plastic bag, but he lifted the other to point at his son. "Stop faffing with your mates and get your lazy rear home. I told you to tidy the flat."

While Shaun stared at his dad, Bren caught something in his expression he'd never seen there before. Something uneasy and sour. But when Shaun's eyes met Bren's, his face hardened and he pulled back his head. "I'll do it later. Got stuff to do."

"No you bloody haven't."

Shaun's dad was heading towards them, crossing the road with the aggressive swagger that never seemed to leave him. Bren's mouth felt even drier than before; his tongue was stuck to the roof of his mouth. He'd clocked the scowl on Shaun's dad's face, which was scornful and stubbly beneath black, combed-back hair.

"The only thing *you* need to do," continued his dad, "is clean up that tip, like I told you this morning. But it's in one ear and out the other with you, isn't it?"

Shaun's eyes met Bren's again, causing him to stand taller and push out his lips. "I *said* I'll do it later."

Bren pivoted discreetly on the pavement, trying to slip away. But when he faced the Dale, a harsh caw made him freeze. His eyes darted up and he saw a crow, eyeing him from its perch on a street light ahead.

The sight sucked the breath from Bren's lungs. When he took a step forward the crow cawed again, puffing its feathers and jabbing the air with its beak.

Bren hesitated, turning back and forth between Shaun and the bird. The crow lifted its wings, poised to swoop. Bren turned again, saw Shaun's dad squaring up to his son.

The last time Bren had seen Shaun's dad was a couple of days ago. While walking past the Number Eighty-seven parked at the bus stop, he'd heard someone yelling, and glanced into the bus to see Shaun's dad hassling the driver over fares or something. He was stretching out his stocky neck, so he could jut his head right into the driver's face.

Just like he was doing to Shaun now.

"Giving me lip, are you?"

Shaun flinched as his dad jerked to and fro, feinting left to right like a boxer.

"I said..." Shaun tried to speak firmly, but a hoarseness had crept into his words. "Just...let me do it tonight. In a bit, yeah?"

"Nah." His dad shook his head, stepping back.

Shaun began to glower. "It's not even my mess."

"You what?" The words came quick. Shaun's dad narrowed his eyes. When Bren saw those shoulders rolling beneath his black bomber jacket, he pivoted again, desperate to disappear. Glancing up, he saw with relief that the crow was gone, and began to shuffle away.

"Where d' you think you're off to?"

Bren stopped and turned. Shaun's dad was eyeballing him now, cocking his head and smiling darkly. "You one of Shaun's mates?"

"Um...I..." Bren took a shaky breath. "Sort of?"

"Sort of," scoffed Shaun's dad. He jabbed a finger towards his son. "Shaun here thinks he's tough, doesn't he?"

Bren didn't know what to say. He shrugged with a wince.

Shaun's dad laughed. "I'll bet he does. But let me tell you something. He loves to act all hard and grown up, but he's actually a whiny little turd." He glanced over his shoulder. "Aren't you, Shaun?"

Shaun didn't say anything. He just seemed to tremble – ever so slightly – with his lips taut and his fists clenched.

His dad's eyes were on Bren again. "Don't fall for it. He's a waste of space. Useless at school and even more useless at home. It's embarrassing."

He turned to his son, pulling a face of mock shame. "Sorry, fella. Did I take you down a peg in front of your buddy?" Shaun's dad laughed then and – after jabbing his son's forehead with his finger – made for the grass. Strutting to the tower, he called over his shoulder. "Five minutes, Shaun. If you're not back and starting on that flat by then, I'll make you regret it."

Bren and Shaun watched in terse silence as Shaun's dad continued on his way, a cold gust of wind flapping his grey joggers.

When Shaun turned to Bren he was breathing heavily, as if he couldn't get enough air into his lungs. The flush on his cheeks was fierce against his skin. Bren's mouth fell open; there was a dampness welling in Shaun's eyes.

"Sh-Shaun," he stuttered. "I—"

Before Bren could go on, he'd been knocked to the floor. He clutched his aching stomach, winded and gasping for air.

Shaun glared from above. “If you tell *anyone* about *any* of this…” His shoulders heaved up and down with his breaths. “You’ll know what’s coming.” And with that, he left Bren on the pavement.

Chapter Six

A Ticking Heartbeat

Bren was soon back on Williamsborough Dale, keener than ever to get home. He kept glancing up as he walked, checking the trees and street lights for crows. The thought of those black beaks and talons made him feel physically sick. He could feel the cuts still wet on his fingers, sore and sticking to the inside of his pockets.

A gentle voice said his name.

"Bren?"

Bren peeked sideways and saw Mr Agarwal, who ran the chemist's up the Dale. Bren knew him fairly well from all the times he'd picked up his dad's medication.

Mr Agarwal was handing a hot drink to the homeless woman by the nail salon. She was usually sat there, huddled in her sleeping bag. When Bren saw her watching him, he noticed from her eyes that she was way younger than he'd realized. She looked like she'd barely finished school.

"Hi, Mr Agarwal," said Bren. He kept moving, determined not to stop.

Mr Agarwal called after him. "You okay, my boy?"

"Fine."

The girl called out too. "You sure 'bout that? You're shaking!"

"Just the cold," replied Bren. He almost hugged himself, but had to keep his cuts hidden in his coat. The last thing he wanted was any fuss.

"Bit shy, is he?" he heard the girl murmur.

A sigh from Mr Agarwal. "Wasn't always like that. Went into his shell after what happened with his sister."

"What happened to her?"

Not wanting to hear more, Bren picked up his pace. While crossing Bradbury Avenue he glanced down its length. It may have been a street of weeds, boarded windows and rusting satellite dishes, but it was a welcome sight; the next street along was Herbert Road. Bren was nearly home.

There used to be a knocker on the front door of forty-seven Herbert Road, but it snapped off a few months ago and was never replaced. All that was left now was its brass plate and broken hinge.

Bren eased a hand carefully from his coat, hissing as his cuts grazed the lining of his pockets. After finding his key and opening the door, he glimpsed Dad in the hallway and thrust his hand back into his coat.

Dad came to the door. A smile took shape beneath his hooked nose.

"Hey, matey. You alright?"

"Yeah."

His dad nodded. After scratching his greying mop of hair, he stepped aside to let Bren in. Bren brushed past, kicking off his shoes and heading straight up the stairs.

Dad called timidly after him. "You want a snack or something?"

"Nah."

"You not taking your coat off?"

"Upstairs."

"Gotcha." His dad seemed to hesitate. Bren could hear him shifting on his feet in the hallway. "Your mum'll be late back tonight. She's got to work overtime."

"Okay."

"She says she's sorry she's been working late so much. You know how she—"

"I know, it's okay."

"Alright, son."

Bren took the corner at the top of the stairs, paused, then turned around to peek back down. Dad was gone, so he crept across the landing – past the rip in the carpet that had never been fixed – to his parents' bedroom, which was opposite the top of the staircase.

Like the rest of Bren's house, his parents' room was

immaculately clean, though the furniture was suffering from wear and tear. With his hands still in his duffel coat, Bren went to his mum's bedside table and gazed down at Evie's urn.

Its beige, polished marble looked expensive. His parents had bought the urn when they were both still working, before his dad took bereavement leave from his job and never went back.

A framed photo was propped next to the urn. It showed Evie sat barefoot outside the family tent, grinning in sunlight and wearing the very watch that was now in Bren's pocket. Her hair and freckles were bright against the tent's blue and grey.

That picture was ten months old now. Evie wasn't quite as tall in it as she was in Furthermoor. And her hair was shorter, her face a tad rounder.

It was one of the last photos ever taken of her, two days before she was hit by a car on the Dale.

Bren slumped on the edge of the bed, his eyes never leaving the framed picture. Not far from that tent was the forest where they'd thought up Furthermoor. The family were spending Easter at a campsite in the Peak District, and while exploring the neighbouring woods, Bren and Evie found a wide, quiet glade. A huge tree straddled a hillock at the glade's edge, with some of its roots framing a burrow in the knoll.

When he wasn't playing football with the kids at the campsite, Bren sometimes joined Evie at the glade so they could read together. Evie had taken a real liking to the big tree – the "tunnel tree", as she called it. On their last day in the glade, Evie noticed that her watch had stopped. It was an old thing she'd spotted in a junk shop the year before; the cogs in its face caught her eye, and she begged Mum and Dad for it for her birthday. She'd never seen a watch's mechanism before and had always loved figuring out how things work. She used to talk about studying engineering after school, and the watch sparked an interest in all things clockwork – so much so that Dad couldn't return from a work trip without bringing back some tin, wind-up animal toy, which she'd proceed to take apart and put together again.

"Uh oh," she'd said in the glade, tapping her birthday watch. "My watch has died. What's the time?"

Bren checked his phone. "Nearly twelve. Better head back for lunch."

Evie pushed her lips out while winding up the watch. As she adjusted its hands, a flower-scented gust swept through the woods, rippling the bluebells between the trees.

Bren watched the flowers settle before turning his head to Evie. "Was that you?" he joked.

Evie wriggled her eyebrows. "Course it was."

"I didn't know your watch was magic."

Evie tutted. "Don't be daft. Magic's not real." She gave a crafty smile. "This is engineering. It's all controlled by cogs and stuff. Watch this."

She looked to and fro, searching the forest. Her gaze rose up the tunnel tree's trunk, and Bren peered where she nodded to see a pink-breasted bullfinch on a branch. The moment it gave a small shriek and launched itself into the air, Evie gave her watch an exaggerated tweak.

"You see," she said, beaming smugly. "This watch controls the woods – even the animals. They're my clockwork creations. You knew that, didn't you?"

Evie was as practical as she was prone to nonsense. It was one of the quirks Bren loved most about her. He'd rolled his eyes at the time, but on the night after Evie was cremated, he lay in their room with the watch held to his chest, watching her empty bed and remembering how she'd joked about the woods. And while thinking about her joke, he put the watch to his ear, listening to its ticking heartbeat. He couldn't kid himself about turning back time, but as he dried his eyes and drifted off to sleep, he imagined a mechanical forest of wood and cogs, crystal and glass. A place that would be safer – cleaner, simpler, easier – than real life. A place where every little thing could be controlled by Evie's watch, just like she'd said.

A place where he could be with his sister, and that was every bit as beautiful as she deserved.

Furthermoor.

Back on his parents' bed, Bren yawned and rubbed his face. Cary. Crows. Shaun and his dad... It had been a long day.

With a sigh, he heaved himself up, went to the bathroom and pulled his hands gently from his coat. He turned on the tap, and watched the water brown and redden while he washed his wounds. When he was done, he returned to the landing, went to his room and closed the door.

Bren's bedroom was pretty bare. It had been that way since Evie's things were moved to the loft. He and Evie used to share this space, since there were only two bedrooms in the house. There'd been plans to move somewhere bigger; the room was getting too small for both of them, and Evie was too old to share. But in the end there were just the three of them, and less money coming in too, what with Dad not working. So the family stayed put on Herbert Road.

Now the room had only Bren's bed and a desk and wardrobe from Ikea, all with their veneer now peeling at the edges. A couple of rock bands sneered from posters on the walls – bands Bren hadn't listened to in months.

It may have been stark, but Bren loved this room. He'd practically grown up in it with his sister. It had everything he needed. Just him, his privacy and Evie's watch.

Letting his backpack and coat slip to the floor, Bren reached into his pocket for the watch. But then he stopped himself, glanced at his school backpack and groaned. Furthermoor would have to wait.

He sat glumly on his chair for some time, staring blankly at the cover of *Animal Farm*. A notepad was open on his desk, with Mr Okorafor's essay question scrawled at the top of the page: *"Power tends to corrupt and absolute power corrupts absolutely." How does this statement relate to the novel?*

Bren's pen fell from his hand. He couldn't be bothered. There was too much he needed to talk about with Evie. Besides, there'd be time for the essay later. He'd probably be more inspired after dinner.

Bren knew he was kidding himself, but he left the desk anyway, throwing himself onto the bed and pulling out Evie's watch. He lifted it to his head and allowed its gentle ticking rhythm to pulse against his ear – to slow his breaths and mellow his heart.

Tick.

Tock.

Tick.

Tock.

A muffled wooden clattering from the wardrobe. Getting up, Bren opened its doors in time to see its floor folding away. Sunlight and scents of sandalwood filled the musty space. Pushing aside clothes on coat hangers, Bren clambered through the wardrobe's base and onto the branches waiting below.

The tree had risen up from a bright bed of jewels. The bordering forest unfurled into the distance, broken to the east by the lake's crystal blue.

Bren opened the watch and flicked some cogs, causing the tree to corkscrew slowly into the ground. Impatient to get to Evie, he clambered down branches while the tree sank and turned. The hole in the sky above him – with its shirts and jumpers all hanging in gloom – was soon lost behind crystal leaves.

As the rumbling tree began to slow, Bren dropped from a branch into a meadow wild with colour. Stained-glass flowers stood tall on their stems. The sun sent its glare through foxgloves and thistles, bluebells and honeysuckles – Evie's favourite blooms in a land without season that had never known clouds.

Glass petals cast rainbows into the air, causing Bren to shade his eyes. It was all a bit *too* bright. A bit too busy. So he took out the watch and adjusted more cogs. With each tweak, the sun lowered a little more, dimming the sky from blue to blue-grey, and causing a pink glow to settle above the distant treetops.

He called across the meadow.

"Evie?"

"Over here!"

She sounded near. Bren adjusted the watch's wheels while he walked. Cables churned within grooves beneath the flora, causing tall wild flowers to part before him – a path straight to his sister.

He found her lounging in a small clearing, twirling a blue flower between her finger and thumb.

"Hey, big sis."

"Hey, little bro."

Bren was already feeling a bit better. He managed to smile at the glass blossom. "Forget-me-not."

"Yup." Evie's eyes went to her brother. "How's it going?"

Bren sighed, then nodded at the trees bordering the meadow. "You fancy a walk?"

"Not great, then."

"Is it obvious?"

"You're doing your grumpy forehead thing. Come on. Let's go."

They walked together through poppies and daffodils, orchids and cowslip – a glimmering meadow of nodding jewels – and entered the forest.

The woods were dusky with the sun so low, but Bren kept it that way. There was something soothing about the softness of the light. As he strolled he saw ferns adjusting to the twilight, rolling up their crystal fronds.

The siblings' pace slowed while Bren told Evie what had happened since he'd last seen her. Mr Okorafor's little talk in the corridor. Cary getting involved by the lockers.

Helping that bird on the road and getting attacked by crows. Shaun and his dad by Ballard Tower.

"Yikes." Evie puffed out a long breath. "That's a rough day."

"Tell me about it. And there'll be more to come. Shaun's not done with me. Not yet. He's really peeved now, and it's all thanks to Cary." He grimaced and threw his hands into the air. "I mean, who does Cary think he is, messing things up like this?"

Smiling gently, Evie put a hand on her brother's arm. "Chill out, little bro. He was only trying to help."

"Well, he's done exactly the opposite. Things were *fine* before he came along."

Evie's eyebrows sank. Bren saw her smile edge towards a frown.

"What?" he asked. The word came out shriller than he'd intended. "What's that look for?"

Evie shrugged, straightening her glasses. "I guess things were…sort of fine. Depends on how happy you were to be…you know…" She looked uncomfortable and began fidgeting with the waist of her summer dress.

Bren's lips clenched. "No," he finally said. "I don't know. Happy to be what?"

Evie shrugged again. "You know… Keeping to yourself the way you do. Staying out of things."

"What's wrong with that?"

"You don't really...*like* it that way, do you? You used to hang out with your friends all the time."

Bren searched for words. "I..."

The truth was that he used to love being with his friends. But after Evie's death they became so awkward around him. Sure, there was kindness there – they really cared. But there was a grating kind of pity too, which made Bren feel low, feeble, ungrateful. He started spending time alone after that, hiding at home or in the music room.

It was only natural that his friends drifted away. Bren didn't blame them. And in some ways, it didn't matter; he was happier in Furthermoor. Happier with Evie.

"Hey." Evie tapped his arm. "You get lonely sometimes, right? I mean, why else would you come here so much?"

"I come here to...to see you."

"Well yeah. Sure. But you don't need to. I'm fine by myself."

Bren flinched at Evie's words; she couldn't have known how much they stung. With a hard shake of his head, he shifted the subject. "And anyway, what did Cary mean when he said he didn't realize Shaun had...someone like me? Going on like he knows what he's talking about."

Evie opened her mouth to reply, but was interrupted by a grinding noise from nearby. The siblings turned their heads, following the coarse, erratic sound. It was getting louder. Something was moving nearby, glinting between tree trunks.

When it came closer, Bren spotted the jewelled fan of a peacock's tail. But something was wrong. The mechanical bird had lost its proud strut and instead hobbled in a lurching limp. It parted its beak and let out a distorted, honking cry. The sound sent goosebumps prickling across Bren's skin. It sounded so pained, so broken – so foreign to Furthermoor.

He opened the watch while moving cautiously towards the peacock. With the twist of some cogs, the ivy on a nearby tree lit up like a coil of fairy lights, casting a green glow that illuminated the bird's feathers. Its fan-like plumage – a mosaic of gemstones – flashed and trembled.

With nausea pinching his stomach, Bren crouched to calm the peacock. He shuddered when he saw what was wrong. A clump of blue silk and white stuffing had been ripped from its thigh.

"But how…?" Bren's voice was trembling. Peering through the gnarly gap in the bird's wire frame, he saw the damaged gears and sprockets that were causing the peacock to limp.

Evie came closer. She put a hand to her mouth when she saw the exposed, twisted wire. "Oh god…" The peacock jerked its head towards her, causing the sapphires on its crest to shudder. It honked again, its topaz eyes twinkling with fear.

"This can't be right," said Bren. "It's not possible. Not... here."

He was studying the watch's cogs, preparing to repair the bird, when Evie gasped his name.

Bren looked up, saw her staring off into the woods. "What is it?"

Her hand rose slowly. When Bren followed her finger he saw something – something dark and larger than any of Furthermoor's creatures – moving through the distant canopy, flitting between branches in the peacock's wake.

Bren got to his feet. The forest felt darker, somehow. His eyes flickered between the thing in the trees and the cogs in the watch.

The blood drained from his face. "Something's wrong," he croaked. "That thing, heading this way... Whatever it is...I didn't make it. It shouldn't be here."

Evie's forehead creased. "Then how's it—"

"I don't know." Bren's words were breathless, panicked. "This should all be under...under control. Under *my* control. It can't be happening."

Chapter Seven

Beak and Feather

Evie took Bren's hand. The thing was getting closer. It shook each branch as it went, causing cables and wood to creak and groan. When it was right above them, Bren arched his neck and pulled Evie back.

The peacock shrieked and fled, grinding and limping with its damaged leg. Its folded tail dragged across wool-moss.

Bren squinted up into the tree, but it was too dark to see. He adjusted some wheels in the watch, and a quiet buzzing filled the undergrowth.

The foliage was soon lit by a skittering green glow. Mechanized fireflies zipped to and fro, repelling the darkness with the bulbs on their tiny copper abdomens. Bren guided them up the tree he was peering into, so that they illuminated its lichen and pulleys.

Then he saw it. A large silhouette, crouched between gears on a thick branch.

"Evie," he whispered. "You see it?"

Evie nodded. "It's watching us."

Bren was scared, but he told himself he shouldn't be. He was safe. He was in Furthermoor. He had the watch.

Pushing out his jaw, he took a step forward and shouted into the tree. "I can see you, you know! Whatever you are, come down! Stop hiding!"

The crouching shape shifted in firefly light. And then, with a clumsy thrashing of wings, it descended.

Bren stumbled backwards as the creature hit the floor. The last thing he'd expected was for it to look so...*human*.

Even though it squatted on the moss with its arms between its knees, Bren could tell it was roughly his height, perhaps a little shorter. But it was definitely scrawnier. Its crooked, stick-like legs were swaddled in the skinniest black jeans, and its ash-grey feet were naked, thin and long, like the bare feet of some bloodless clown.

Compared to its gaunt legs and feet, the creature's black hoodie was lumpen and baggy. In the pulsing green light, Bren saw that its bony black wings – now folded tightly behind the faded hoodie – were shabby and short of feathers.

Bren glanced at Evie. Her gaping eyes were fixed on the creature's pulled-up hood, which was unlike anything Bren had ever seen. The fabric towards its top gave way to scuffed, black scales, and its peak extended outwards in a sharp, curving point – like a steely beak hanging over the creature's face.

Bren couldn't see its features. Even in the fireflies' light, the darkness within that hood was thick, inky, impenetrable.

The thing gibbered and hopped forward, causing Bren to step back again. He yanked Evie's hand, pulling her with him, all the while with his eyes on the creature.

It crooked its neck, taking the siblings in with tiny movements of its hood. And Bren noticed that, even though it moved in twitches, the motions weren't mechanical at all. They were organic, furtive, sly. This creature was no machine.

Evie whispered to Bren: "What is it?"

Bren was about to reply – to say he had no idea – but the creature spoke first.

"Good question. What am I?" Its voice was coarse as bark, dusty as death.

Bren's eyes narrowed. This...*thing* had no right to be here. A flush of anger overcame his fear. He stepped forward, leaning a little to look down upon the creature.

It aimed its hidden face at him. That beaked hood twitched minutely in all directions, as if the creature couldn't keep its head still.

"You tell me," demanded Bren. "What are you?"

"No-no-no, *you* tell *me*," came a creak of a reply. "You

made me, did you not?" The thing ruffled its tattered wings, glanced about the clearing. "That'sssss how things work here, isn't it?"

Slowly but with certainty, Bren shook his head. "I made all this, but I didn't make you. Who are you?"

"You'd like a name, little imagineer?"

"It'd be a start."

"Then give me one. You thought me up. You can at least name me."

"I *didn't* make you." Bren held up his watch, pointing at the cogs. "You're nothing to do with me!"

The creature hopped backwards, cackled and belched. "I'm sure I'm *everything* to do with you. And there's no need for anger, young lord of this land. Don't resent me. I didn't ask to exist. It's you who brought me here."

"Didn't you hear me? I said—"

"That you didn't make me, yes-yes-yes. But use the grey lump in your fancy-filled head. You *must* have made me. For where else could I come from? A part of you created me, whether you wanted it to or not."

"That's stupid. I know what I want to imagine. And I didn't imagine you!"

The thing wagged a skinny grey finger. "Imagination's not so easily tamed. Imagination sets its own rules, has a l-life of its own. It doesn't always do as it's told."

A dry, cawing cackle. "As a child you feared the monsters

beneath your bed, did you not? It took many a year to *un*-imagine them. There's no easy exile of the beasts of the mind. So, no – imagination cannot be c-conquered. Not entirely. It is a free and savage thing."

The creature chittered and wheezed. "And since imagination takes liberties, I'll take the liberty of imagining myself a name. A name such as…Fevvers?" It shook its hood. "Not quite right. How about…Featherly? Featherrrrrly." A sharp nodding. "Yes-yes-yes, Featherly it is."

Bren was grimacing at his watch, searching desperately for any cogs that tallied with this creature. He flashed the mechanism at Evie. "It's not showing here. I can't get rid of it!"

A dry clacking from Featherly – something between a laugh and a tut. He rose slowly from his haunches, standing almost as tall as Bren. "Imagination does as it pleases. Young master's not the master he thinks he is."

Bren's eyes were on Featherly. He pointed into the darkness. "So that was you?"

"What was me, young lord?"

"The peacock. Did you damage it?"

Featherly fell silent, then let out a dry belch. A puff of white stuffing flew out from his hood, before drifting gently onto the wool-moss below. A shrug of that black baggy hoodie. "One of many."

Bren's eyes widened. "*Many?*"

"A squirrel here, a hare there. Perhaps a fox or two. All the same inside, though." Featherly reached into his hoodie's front pocket. He pulled out a handful of springs, gears and sprockets, which he threw at Bren's feet.

Bren almost gagged at the sight of the twinkling metal. Evie must have sensed his horror. She came close and he felt her palm on his back.

Evie eyed Featherly quizzically. "But why?" she asked, sounding far calmer than Bren felt. "Why are you hurting the animals?"

Featherly patted his chest. "As well as putting breath in these lungs, the young lord's been kind enough to give me hunger."

"Hunger?"

Featherly shuddered, shaking his featherbare wings. "*Meat,*" he rasped. "I need meat and I'm famished. Can you imagine how it is, to pine for flesh where there's only cogs? To crave the bonely crunch – the taste of tendon and muscle – when all around there's nothing but rivets and wire?"

He lowered his head and shook his shoulders, making a weeping sound as feeble as it was sly. But he stopped abruptly, jerking his head up to the siblings. Bren caught the flash of eyes within that hood.

"But what about you?" whispered Featherly, pointing a bone-like finger between Evie and Bren. "You're not fashioned from cogs and cotton, are you?" He shuffled forward, sniffing and chattering. "Is that meat I smell? Does hot blood flow beneath that freckled flesh?"

Bren glanced at Evie, who didn't look frightened at all; more intrigued than anything else. But he put himself between the creature and his sister.

Featherly chortled. "Fret not, little fleshlings; I'd never gobble you up. I'm no monster." Another dry laugh. "Besides, human meat is foul."

The tip of his hood rose, as if he were looking down his nose at Bren. "But just look at you, the little lord, prancing to your sister's aid. How noble. At least you have some backbone *here*."

Bren scowled. "What's that supposed to mean?"

"You're not so blessed with courage when it comes to… Shaun, was it? Is that the boy's name?"

Bren's chin dropped. "How… How do you know about that?"

"I've dropped eaves, young lord. I've heard you gripe to your sister. Whine-whine-whine, snivel-snivel-snivel."

"How dare—"

"And I must say," cawed Featherly, pushing on, "that this Cary speaks truth."

The muscles in Bren's jaw tightened. His words came out low, forced between rigid lips. "What are you talking about?"

"You're letting yourself down, young fleshling. A master in this realm, a runt in the other."

"You can't—"

"I know *exactly* what Cary means when he says 'someone like you'. You're a whipping boy, young master." Featherly's voice was coarsening, fraying even more at its edges. "A sitting target. A willing sacrifice."

Bren felt his face flush red. His wrists ached from the clenching of his fists. "How dare you say that! Who do you—"

"A feeble dog," rasped Featherly, his dry voice rising, "that accepts its kicking, every single time."

Bren's mouth twisted but no words came.

Featherly's ragged wings began to part, opening further with every word. "A coward and a skulk. A living doormat. A lure for violence. A—"

"*Stop it!*" It was Evie. She was trembling by Bren's side. "This is horrible! Just stop saying these things! Stop it right now!"

Featherly squawked a cackling, rasping laugh. With a flap of those moulting wings, he launched himself onto a branch above, before darting back the way he'd come.

Bren could only stare while Featherly's silhouette dwindled, flapping gracelessly from tree to tree. Crystal leaves chimed in the distance.

Finally finding his tongue, Bren cried out after

Featherly. "You don't know what it's like!" Hot tears began to brim in his eyes. He lowered his voice. "You can't just… *choose* to be brave."

His voice broke on the last word. When Evie took him in her arms, he pushed his head into her shoulder.

"It's okay," she hushed.

"What does he know? He's a *freak*. A weirdo with feathers." Bren pulled away to peer into the woods. "And where is he now? He calls me a coward, then runs away into the trees."

The siblings gazed up into the canopy. The fireflies had scattered, leaving the leaves more black than green, like curls of smoked glass.

And then they heard a woman's voice, calling faintly on the breeze.

Bren let out a groan. "It's Mum. I'd better go back." He stayed where he was though, frowning at the gloom.

"What are you waiting for?" asked Evie.

Bren eyed the forest. "He's still out there somewhere." He took his sister's hand. "I'm sort of…worried about leaving you. You know, with that Featherly thing around."

Evie let out a genuine laugh. "You can hardly take me with you, can you? And you need to go back. If you don't snap out of your daydream up there, Mum's gonna freak out and think you're in a coma or something."

Bren sighed. "Yeah. I know. But…" He was still scanning

the trees, searching for signs of Featherly. "We don't know anything about him. I don't know what he's...capable of."

Evie gave him a shove. "Don't you dare patronize me, little brother. I can look after myself. I'm not scared of that...thing, whatever it is."

Mum's voice came on the wind again, prompting Bren to tweak some cogs in his watch. The nearest tree began to turn, parting the canopy to reveal a dusky sky.

"Okay." Before he could think twice, Bren hugged his sister and pulled awkwardly away. "Look after yourself. I'll be back as soon as I can."

"Don't rush, Bren. Spend some time with Mum and Dad."

Bren didn't reply. He was already climbing.

Chapter Eight
Fuss

Tock.

Tick.

Tock.

Tick.

A blink of his eyes and the bedroom was dark. Bren must have been in Furthermoor for some time. The only light came from the street lights outside his window, and from the open bedroom door.

And there was Mum, leaning through the doorway in her office skirt and blouse, with the light from the landing spilling over her shoulders.

"Bren?"

Bren blinked again, then rolled on the bed to squint at her silhouette. "Yeah?"

"I said dinner's waiting."

"What time is it?"

"Just gone nine."

Bren sat up. "Seriously?" His eyes flitted to the unwritten essay on his desk. "Why didn't Dad get me down earlier?"

"He came up to call but you didn't answer. When he popped his head in, you were chilling or something. Daydreaming."

"He could still have got me down."

A hint of terseness crept into Mum's voice. "He wasn't keen on bothering you, Bren. Last time he interrupted you – you know, staring into space – you got a bit…cross with him."

Bren was on his feet, following his mum onto the landing. "I didn't get cross," he mumbled. "It's not like I shouted or had a go at him."

"No, but you were a bit ratty. And you know your dad's…" Her words trailed off. Glancing down the staircase, she lowered her voice. "You know he's a bit… sensitive. So give him a break. He was just trying to be considerate. Okay?"

Mum's big hazel eyes were on him. They were so much like Evie's.

Bren searched his mum's face. Seeing her so fresh from Furthermoor, he realized – with a dull pang in his chest – how much Evie was growing up to look like Mum. Evie would never be older than thirteen – not here, in real life –

but in Furthermoor she was nearly a year older. Her face was taking on the same shape as Mum's. Her freckled cheekbones were sharper now, her chin narrowing. She had Dad's nose, but it was less beakish on her than it was on Bren.

"What's wrong?" Mum looked concerned. "What's that look for?"

"What look?"

"So...sad." Mum's expression grew sombre with the words. She shifted uneasily on the stairs.

Bren shrugged. "I'm fine." He lowered his eyes to his hands and regretted it instantly.

Mum followed his gaze and her face hardened. "And what's *this*?" She frowned at the cuts on his palms, which must have bled a little while Bren was in Furthermoor. "What happened?" Mum took his wrists gently so she could angle the cuts towards the light on the landing.

"It's nothing."

"Doesn't look like nothing."

"I fell in the playground. Playing football at lunchtime. It's no big deal."

"Come downstairs. We'll get those cleaned up." She turned and continued down the staircase.

Bren trudged after her, heading for the front room while his mum went to the kitchen.

Falling back onto a sofa, Bren rolled his eyes at the

reality show on TV, where an orange couple were squabbling and flashing pouts at each other. His eyes drifted to the mantelpiece above the gas fire, which must have been there since the 1980s. The mantel was crammed with photos of Evie, along with the clockwork animals she'd dismantled and repaired. Tin frogs and butterflies and wind-up mice. A metal hen and mechanical fish. The bickering on TV faded to background noise.

Dad had moved Evie's animals downstairs just after she'd died. Bren often caught him lingering by them when he was dusting. He'd brush their felt and tin softly with his fingertips, sometimes even lifting them to his cheek. This was the complete opposite of Mum, who – as far as Bren could tell – tried to pretend they weren't even there.

The sound of hard footsteps pulled Bren from his thoughts. Mum marched through the door, armed with antiseptic wipes, creams and plasters. After turning down the TV, she kneeled by Bren and pulled up his palms.

"Playing football," she muttered, tearing out a wipe and dabbing his cuts. "I wish that school would let you play on the field at lunchtime. The concrete's hardly ideal, is it? The amount of times you've come home with bumps and grazes..."

Bren had to look away, so he turned his head to the framed photos on the wall behind the armchair. One of them had been taken several years ago, on the beach at

Scarborough. There was Dad's face, barely in shot while he tried to take the selfie, with his hair black and short, smiling a smile Bren hadn't seen in months. Mum on a towel, laughing in her sunglasses, sunburned but happy. Evie – Mum's miniature clone – in her frilly swimsuit, only half looking at the camera, her attention still on the elaborate moat she was digging around her sandcastle. And Bren in neon Bermuda shorts – probably no older than five – frozen by the camera in a glorious star jump, his red hair salty and wet.

"Morning, Bren," joked Dad, entering the front room with a plate of lasagne in each hand. Bren glanced away from the picture, saw his dad flinch as if regretting the tease.

Bren spoke softly. "Sorry I didn't come down, Dad. Lost track of time."

Dad eased a plate onto the carpet close to where Bren was sitting, and rested the other on the floor a little further down the sofa. "No worries." He smiled vaguely at Bren, but frowned when he saw his wife putting a plaster on the first of Bren's grazes. "What happened to your hands?"

"It's nothing," said Bren again. The words came automatically – more a reflex than a reply.

"He fell while he was playing football," answered Mum, turning curtly to her husband. "Didn't you notice when he got home?"

"I..." spluttered Bren's dad, his eyes darting about the room. "It..."

"It's not Dad's fault," said Bren. "I had my hands in my pockets. Dad wouldn't have seen."

Mum's eyes narrowed. "Then why didn't you tell him so he could patch you up?"

Dad scarpered out of the room – presumably to get the last plate of lasagne, but no doubt gratefully fleeing the scene.

Bren gave the usual shrug, with his eyes low, while Mum stood up. "Didn't want a fuss," he said.

Mum didn't reply, but Bren could feel her watching him. He kept his gaze on the toys on the mantelpiece, already itching to be back in Furthermoor.

Mum sighed, her voice softening. "You never do want a fuss, do you, Bren?"

Bren shrugged again, but was forced to meet Mum's eyes when she returned to her knees and used a finger to lift his chin. She smiled tiredly. "You're worth a fuss, Bren. You know that, don't you?"

Bren swallowed, nodding with Mum's finger still under his chin.

"Don't ever forget it." Mum's palm was on his cheek now. She ran her fingers tenderly through his hair. "Me and Dad worry about you sometimes, you know? We've not seen much of you lately. You're always in your room."

"You're always at work."

Mum winced, took a deep breath and carried on. "Tonight's not the first time I've found you lying around just staring at the ceiling. Why don't you try getting out a bit more?"

Bren pulled his head back from her hand. "Nothing to do."

"There's plenty. You used to play football by the tower all the time. Why not now?"

"Too cold."

"That never stopped you before."

Bren shrugged.

"If it's cold, you can go to your friends' houses," persisted Mum. "Or have them round here. Do some gaming or something."

"I'll think about it."

Thin lips from Mum. "You always say that."

"I'm still thinking about it."

Mum huffed lightly, took her plate from the carpet and sat at the other end of the sofa.

Bren put his own plate on his lap and hacked at his lasagne. When he forked some into his mouth, he saw the plasters on his hands and thought with a shudder about the crows that had attacked him earlier.

He closed his eyes and flinched, remembering the thrash of black feathers. And then he thought of Featherly. He had to get back to Furthermoor. He had to know Evie was okay.

Mum was pushing her lips out, deep in thought. That was where Evie got it from.

"Bren," she began. "I have to ask… You'd tell us if something was bothering you, wouldn't you?"

Bren nodded vaguely, grabbed the remote and turned up the TV. Again, he could feel Mum watching him, and when he clocked Dad hovering awkwardly with his food by the door – probably waiting for this conversation to end – he was reminded of why he never told his parents anything. He remembered the mess they'd been in for months after they lost Evie – the mess they were pretty much still in, though Mum hid it better than Dad.

Bren stared at his food. As if he could really whine to them about Shaun, school work and crows. They had enough to deal with. More than enough.

He raised his eyes to the door and sighed. "You coming in, Dad?"

His dad cringed, nodded and crossed the room, before easing himself carefully into the armchair. He always moved so gingerly, as if a slip or bump might dent him.

After clearing his throat, Dad pushed out a loud, exaggerated sigh; a blatant attempt to clear the air. He smiled at Bren. "So how was school, matey? Anything interesting happen?"

Bren chewed silently on his reheated lasagne, thinking back to the school corridor – to Shaun's hands pinning his shoulders; to the hardness of metal lockers against his back; to Cary and his meddling.

He shook his head with his eyes on his food. "Nah. Just another day."

PART THREE
TUESDAY

CHAPTER NINE

WALK AWAY

The following afternoon found Bren on Williamsborough Dale, with hood up and eyes down, crunching through the thick snow that had fallen that morning. He plodded and shivered, homeward bound after the school bell's final ring.

He'd been careful in the classrooms and corridors. He'd been vigilant. He'd stuck to the fringes and stayed out of harm's way. He'd kept his head low and his mouth shut. And he'd been rewarded with an uneventful day.

Sure, he'd accidentally met Cary's eyes in English class. But the look on Cary's face had been friendly. So genuinely friendly, in fact, that Bren struggled to send back a grimace and almost smiled in return. During lunchtime he'd had to sit in detention and blag that essay for Mr Okorafor. It hurt – as in, almost physically – to miss out on the arts block and Furthermoor. But things could have been worse.

At least with Mr Okorafor he was safe from Shaun.

While Bren shuffled along the Dale, past roads of grey slush and pavements blanketed white, he eyed the street lights and trees – which were thankfully crow-free – and thought about last night. His mum hadn't fussed any more over him, thank god; she'd had a glass of wine with dinner, which always helped her chill out. After finishing his lasagne, Bren had gone straight back to his room, and returned to the forest beneath his wardrobe to find no trace of Featherly.

He was grateful for that, but uneasy too. What if Featherly was still in Furthermoor somewhere, damaging more animals?

And what was he, anyway? Where did he come from?

Bren stumbled over a fast-food carton jutting from the snow, still deep in thought. Maybe Featherly had been some sort of random, fleeting creation – a temporary blip of his imagination, prompted by that crow attack. Bren seriously hoped so. Just the thought of Featherly – with his scaly hood and scabby wings – was sickening.

He'd just passed the shops when he heard someone shriek.

Bren stopped in his tracks. It wasn't a full cry; more a voice cut off mid-howl. An animal noise caught between rage and fear.

He turned to see where the sound had come from, and

found himself looking down Bradbury Avenue, with its boarded windows and barred-up doors; its snow-topped nettles and rusting road signs.

And there, at the road's far end, small with distance: a glimpse of Cary being dragged out of sight, with what looked like someone's hand over his mouth.

Bren's lips parted silently, and his chest stung with the cold air sucked into his lungs. That hand was Shaun's. It had to be. He must have been itching to teach Cary a lesson.

Shaun never forgets.

Never.

Bren glanced quickly about, in case anyone else had heard or seen. There were a couple of younger school kids across the road, on the avenue's other corner where it met the Dale. They were staring at the spot where Cary had been, but the moment they saw Bren watching, they exchanged glances and – coming to some unspoken agreement – feigned confusion and peered in every direction but Bradbury Avenue.

Bren looked on, stunned, while they shrugged at each other – as if giving up on some minor mystery – then turned away and continued across the snow.

He was tempted to do the same. The next street along was Herbert Road. He could cross the avenue, carry on a little further, turn right and be home. Away from this. Warm, safe and sound.

Someone else would help Cary. Someone braver.

But that's what those kids across the road must have told themselves, right?

Bren watched the spot where Cary had disappeared, willing him to appear again; to outfox Shaun and come running up the road. But nothing happened.

He peered about again. Cars were crawling along the main road, their drivers' faces vacant and fixed ahead. A pair of schoolgirls on the Dale's other side were walking while scrolling through their phones. Bren could chase them, tell them what he'd seen. But as he flexed to run, he faltered and groaned, fearful at the thought of trying to talk to people he didn't know. What if they ignored him? What if they laughed? What if they thought it was *hilarious* that the ginger loner from school was even looking at them?

Or even worse: what if they believed him but did nothing, just like the two who'd played dumb and walked away?

Bren had seen it a million times. People looking the other way in corridors and toilets – turning a blind eye, just like Cary had said – and leaving him in the clutches of Shaun, Alex and Isaiah. Time and time again.

Not that Bren blamed them. And now *he* could be on the side that looks away, safely on the fringes. He could convince himself that this was someone else's problem –

that someone else would help. He could avert his gaze and keep walking.

But no. He couldn't.

Bren was already moving down Bradbury Avenue. As he tried to force some courage into his step, he thought back to what Evie had said in Furthermoor. Sure, Cary was cocky and full of himself – a meddler doing more damage than he realized. But Evie was right: Cary was only trying to help. He was the only person who – for once – hadn't looked the other way. He'd even tried to be friends.

Whether Bren liked it or not, he owed him.

He was more than halfway down Bradbury Avenue now, skirting weeds and nettles rigid with cold. A rotting sofa lay behind him, half buried in snow.

And then: a harsh caw. A shadow soaring across white.

At the sound of a swooping squawk, Bren dodged instinctively and felt the air swept by wings. Something thumped and scratched his hood, causing him to duck and fall. He stayed on his knees with his head bent low, fearing the slash of beak and claw. But nothing came.

Bren glanced up. The crow was gone. But he faltered then, looking back the way he'd come.

It wasn't too late to turn back. Maybe Cary was okay; he was clever and could look after himself. Or maybe Bren had glimpsed some sort of game. Maybe nothing was even wrong.

Bren sighed and started walking. He was slower now,

his usual stoop and shuffle restored. But he was still heading deeper into the avenue, to where he'd seen Cary pulled from sight.

He wouldn't kid himself. He wouldn't look away. He knew how much that hurt.

As he passed a toppled shopping trolley glazed with ice, Bren slowed even more and clung closer to the terraces. He was nearing the end of the avenue, and roughly in the area where he'd seen Cary snatched away. Most of the doors were bricked or boarded up, so Bren wasn't sure where Cary could have gone.

But then he saw it. The gate between house numbers fifty-nine and sixty-one was hanging open, its rotting wood splintered where the lock had been smashed away.

He crept to the gate, then peered into an alleyway with walls giving way to garden fences.

Bren's heart was beating hard, thumping against his ribs while he skulked through the alley. The snow here was high and hard, and the crunch of Bren's shoes made him wince with every step. He saw deep footprints – from two or three people, by the looks of it – and kicks and gashes in the blue-white ice. Signs of struggle.

Bren paused and reached for his trouser pocket, thinking suddenly of his phone. Why hadn't he thought of it before? He could call the police. They should be doing this, not him.

Bren's hand lingered, though, and he closed his eyes. He couldn't call the police. What would he say? That a school pupil *might* be in trouble? He had no idea what was actually happening here – whether Cary and Shaun were even still around. And if they were, what would Shaun make of Bren calling the police on him? What price would Bren have to pay?

Bren shivered, as much from his thoughts as from the cold. But, with jaw clenched and his hands tucked beneath his armpits, he continued along the alley and found a gate open to the right. Beyond it waited a junkyard that used to be a garden. Bicycle frames, plastic delivery crates, a torn pram. Roof tiles, rotten wood and rubble, piled onto a bed's broken base. And all of it peeking out from a thick coat of snow.

Bren heard something. It came faintly from the back door, which had been knocked open like the gate to the alley. Music. Bass-heavy beats and speed-of-light lyrics, spat out and storming. And bursts of laughter, cutting through the rhythm.

Bren knew that sound. The hyena cackles of Isaiah and Alex.

He considered the open back door. Bradbury Avenue's terraces were just like the ones on Herbert Road. This house had the same layout as Bren's. And he could tell that the noise came from deeper in the building – probably the living room, close to the front door. That meant the kitchen beyond the back door should be empty.

Should be.

Clinging close to the fence, Bren moved through the garden and peered past the door frame. The kitchen was empty. Its ancient white cooker – now scarred with pocks and rust – leaned at a crooked angle from the flaking wall. Above a mould-mottled sink, greasy curtains framed the kitchen window, which allowed only smears of light through its metal grating. Most of the room's light came through the open door, casting a bar of white across the litter on the floor.

Bren lingered by the door. He clenched and unclenched his fingers, tempted again to turn away. But then he remembered how Cary had stood up to Shaun for him, and how he'd invited him to join the crowd in the corridor.

Stepping over the snow on the threshold, Bren entered the house.

Chapter Ten

The Wolf's Lair

Bren moved slowly through the kitchen, setting his wet shoes carefully between rubble, rusting cans and scraps of wallpaper.

It was darker in the hallway, but there was light – and music – coming from the front room, just ahead to the left. Bren was grateful that the music was so loud; it hid his panicked breathing. His heart pounded so hard it seemed to jar against his lungs and shudder his breaths.

Bren pushed a palm against his chest, struck by a thought. Even if he found Cary, what could he possibly do to help him? He hesitated again. Maybe he should get out while he could.

A shake of the head. He should at least find out what was going on here, decide from there. So Bren shuffled forward, before squinting through the gap between the front room's door frame and open door.

And just as expected, there was Shaun.

He was slouching on a tatty office chair near the door, holding court over Alex and Isaiah, who were lounging in puffer jackets on the frayed carpet beyond. Damp plaster glistened behind peeling strips of wallpaper. The floor was littered with empty cans and takeaway boxes.

The music came blaring from a speaker perched on a cardboard box, next to the camping lamp that gave the room most of its light, since the window to the avenue was boarded up. Isaiah and Alex nodded to the beat while Shaun orated from his threadbare throne, waving his hands and telling some story Bren couldn't make out over the music.

So this was the trio's lair. Somewhere to hang out, away from prying eyes. But where was Cary?

He wasn't in the front room. He must have escaped.

Bren winced. He didn't need to be here. He'd taken this ridiculous risk for nothing. He should have just followed his instincts and walked on.

But as Bren retreated from the doorway, he sensed something. A faint, regular trembling in the floorboards – barely noticeable, but distinct from the bass pumped out by the speaker.

He cocked his ear, trying to figure out what was going on.

Then he heard it: a faint pounding, thumping in time

with those trembles in the floor. It was coming from upstairs. Someone was up there.

Cary.

Bren pushed his fingers into his hair. To get upstairs he'd have to get past the front room. Without being seen.

He peered again through the gap. Shaun was still sat with his back to the door; a small blessing. Alex and Isaiah lay facing the doorway, propped on their elbows. But they weren't looking in the door's direction. Isaiah was chuckling with his head tipped back. Alex was smiling at something on his phone.

Before he could change his mind, Bren slipped past the doorway and twisted onto the staircase. Keeping low behind the banister, he slinked his way up and paused when he'd passed the door below, listening out.

The music and guffawing went on, so Bren kept going.

The thumping was more obvious now he was on the stairs. When Bren hit the landing he paused to let his eyes adjust to the gloom, and saw the sound's source. The bedroom door beyond the bathroom was shut but its handle was throbbing. Someone was hitting the door from the inside – probably kicking with their shoes, going by the force of those shudders.

It had to be Cary. Shaun and his lackeys must have locked him in.

Bren crossed the landing to try the door's handle.

The thumping stopped but the door wouldn't budge. The key in its lock resisted Bren's efforts, but after gripping with both hands he managed to twist it. The door still wouldn't move, so Bren tried the key again, jiggling frantically until it jerked and clunked.

This time the door unlocked. When Bren pushed it open he saw Cary recoil in fear. His damp eyes widened with surprise.

"Bren?"

Bren's finger shot to his lips. He glanced at the staircase before whispering, "They're in the front room. We'll have to sneak past them."

Cary – who looked flushed and cold, with his dyed fringe drooping wetly over his brow – nodded and edged forward, desperate to leave the room. Bren caught a glimpse inside. He saw white pricks of sun in the window's metal grating; the dark outline of a mattress, propped against the wall.

Bren led the way, creeping down the stairs and stopping before he was in line with the front-room door. He turned and hissed into Cary's ear, trying to be heard above the music. "Can't see in from here. Don't know if they're watching the doorway. But when they notice you're not banging upstairs, they might come check it out. So we have to go for it. As in, right now." Even in that musty cold, sweat was beading on Bren's forehead. "Are you ready?"

Cary gave a stiff nod. Bren made his move, taking the rest of the steps and turning at the bottom to dart past the front room. The pair of them left the hallway and entered the kitchen, hopping across clutter and escaping into the garden. But then Cary's footsteps stopped.

Bren twisted on the spot. Cary had skidded to a halt amid the snow-topped junk. Bren's fingers clenched in horror. "Why are you *stopping*?"

Cary jerked a thumb at the back door. "Shaun's got my phone. Took it off me before they..." His chin fell.

"*Oi!*" A blast of rage from the hallway – Shaun's voice.

Bren grabbed Cary's arm and they were moving again, fleeing through the garden and alleyway. Snow flew from their feet as they raced up Bradbury Avenue. Bren heard the crunch of shoes, harder and louder as the three boys gained on them.

"And *you*!" Shaun's words cracked the cold air, juddering with his sprinting steps. "*Beakface!* Just wait till I get hold of you!"

Bren lost his footing and nearly stumbled. He could hear from the crunching snow that Shaun was catching up; he was taller, faster, angrier.

"Main road," puffed Cary, pointing ahead. "We'll...be safe there."

"Won't make it," gasped Bren.

They were still at the lower end of the avenue; there was too far to go. Shaun and the others were still gaining. Bren's eyes darted in every direction, before settling on the abandoned sofa just ahead.

"This way," he panted, dashing left into the alley just past the sofa. But he stopped as soon as he was inside, grabbing Cary's arm.

Bewildered, Cary gaped at Bren. "Wha—"

"Get down low," whispered Bren. "Follow me."

Bren led Cary, crawling quickly back out of the alley and into the narrow space between the sofa and brick wall. As they scrabbled along the gap with their hands clawing snow, Bren heard the others tearing past the sofa. Cary stayed close, and they turned the sofa's corner to hide behind its far side, so that they were out of sight while Shaun and the others ran into the alley.

Cary peered over the sofa's snowy arm. "They think we went through the alley," he whispered.

Bren nodded. "They'll be looking for us in the back alleys and gardens now. It'll buy us some time." His eyes rose above the sofa, alongside Cary's. "But not much. We'd better move. Come on. I know somewhere safe."

Chapter Eleven
Clearing

Bren led the way again. They scuttled across snow and ran up the other side of the avenue, before Bren – using weathered brickwork for footing – clambered up a low wall between two houses. He hauled himself over its top and dropped to the ground. Cary landed with a thump beside him, and they crouched together in a clearing beneath bushes and shrubs.

They were quiet for a while. The jittery rise and fall of their chests began to settle.

It was Cary who spoke first. He kept his voice low, while peering through thorns at the wall's crest.

"Wow. You really know your hiding places."

Bren's reply was terse: "What d'you mean by that?"

"No, I mean… It's a good thing. We got away." Cary must have felt safer now; he was trying to smile. But it looked forced, somehow. Strained. "I'm just not so into…

you know…running away from stuff."

"You'd rather be in that room?"

Cary swallowed hard, his eyes misting in the cold. For all his bravado, Bren could see he was scared. And though Bren hated to admit it, he felt a sliver of satisfaction; Cary was human, after all.

Bren bit his lip, ashamed at the feeling, then went on. "That's just the start, you know. They'll do a lot worse than lock you in rooms. Shaun's just getting warmed up. Believe me, I know." He grimaced at the dead leaves by his feet, before looking again at Cary. "What happened? How'd they get you?"

Cary rubbed one of his eyes. "I was just walking home from school. When I reached this road someone called my name. It sounded like a girl – I thought it might be Ava. You know, from Year Nine? So I started walking down here, but after a bit I knew something was up." His expression darkened, though he seemed angrier at himself than anyone else. "Someone pushed me over from behind, and before I knew it, all three of them were dragging me down the road to that…that house."

He shivered then and kneaded his cheeks, as if rubbing away the grime from fifty-nine Bradbury Avenue.

"Shaun went through my pockets and nabbed my phone, and then they shoved me in that room and locked the door. Alex and Isaiah were laughing while Shaun shouted through the keyhole. Said I needed some time to think about my attitude. That's what he called that place: the thinking room.

"When I told him where to go, he said he wouldn't let me out till he heard me...heard me singing..." Cary faltered.

"Singing what?" asked Bren.

Cary's eyes narrowed. "That I'm a takeaway noodle boy." He spat into the dirt. "What a moron. There's no way I'm ever doing that. Not in a million years. I'd rather stay in that room for ever than give in to...to someone like him. Tell you what, though – I got Shaun wrong. I thought he'd back off after I stood up to him yesterday. But Shaun's for real. Like, properly vicious."

After falling silent, Cary turned his face to Bren's. "How far back do you and Shaun go?"

Bren's eyebrows sank. "You make it sound like a relationship."

"Well... It is, in a way."

"You what?"

"Does he have some sort of grudge against you? Or does he just think you're—"

"*Yes*," snapped Bren, keen to stop Cary from elaborating. "He has a grudge. For something that happened ages ago. It wasn't even my fault."

"What was it?" Cary shuffled closer.

Bren bit his bottom lip, remembering how things had got this way. "You know the food bank? Further down the Dale?"

"Yeah, I've seen it."

"A lot of the kids at school – their parents try hard to get work but there's not much going. Nothing solid enough to pay the bills, anyway. And some people can't work for...for other reasons." Bren thought of his dad. "It doesn't mean they're lazy or anything like that."

"Sure." Cary must have sensed the defensiveness in Bren's tone. He tapped the side of Bren's knee with his knuckles. "Hey, I get it. But what's that got to do with Shaun?"

Bren shrugged. "Shaun always used to take the mick out of anyone who used the food bank. Nothing as bad as now, mind. He called them scavs and scroungers – that sort of thing – but he never actually hurt anyone. Not physically. But loads of kids' families use that food bank. Some have to go regularly, you know? So Shaun hurt a lot of people's feelings."

"I bet."

"But Shaun's...a big guy."

"So no one did anything about it."

"Yeah. But one day during last summer holiday, I saw Shaun and his dad come out of the food bank with a bag of cans and stuff."

"No way."

"Yes, way." Bren hugged his knees. "I'd heard before – in the playground – that his parents split up; his mum left home. I mean, there was always talk about his parents. He lives in Ballard Tower, and the kids there said you could always hear the screaming matches between his mum and dad. Or...mostly his dad. He's kind of intense."

"Intense?"

"Put it this way. A while back I saw him having a go at the guy behind the counter in the chippy – like, proper shouting and red in the face – just cos he'd put too much vinegar on his chips."

Cary seemed to be thinking about this. His brow crinkled beneath his dyed fringe. "That might explain some stuff."

"Hm?"

"About Shaun."

Bren chewed his lower lip, remembering how Shaun had been ridiculed by his dad on Lewis Road. "Yeah. Maybe." He puffed a sigh into the chill air. "So, after Shaun's mum left, his dad must've been short of money for food. Plus it was the holidays, so—"

"No school meals."

Bren nodded. "I guess the food bank was Shaun's dad's only option."

Cary was staring glumly at the wall.

"Problem is, though," continued Bren, "when Shaun saw that I'd seen him, he left his dad and stormed right over. Told me I'd better not tell anyone."

"Did he threaten you?"

"Said he'd make me regret it. It was weird, though. He was fuming and stuff, but his eyes kept flicking left and right – in case anyone else had seen, I think. He was proper raging, but he also looked...sort of scared. And sad." Bren held up his hand, pinching his thumb and finger so they almost touched. "I swear he was *this* close to crying."

"He was embarrassed."

"I guess. But mostly angry."

"So what did you do?"

Bren shrugged. "I promised I wouldn't tell anyone."

"But you did tell someone. And then he went on a mission to make your life hell."

"But that's the thing. I *didn't* tell anyone. I knew how much flak he'd get, and there was no way I wanted to stir up trouble. I guess someone else must have seen and told *all* of Williamsborough, cos by the time school started again, everyone was making fun of Shaun. Not in a proper, like, *mean* way. Like I said, loads of families use that food bank. But, you know, after all the fun he'd made of everyone else..."

"They couldn't resist."

"Yeah. Shaun hated it, and that's when he started

getting nasty. Started pushing people over if they looked at him the wrong way, or even punching them. Locking them in toilet cubicles. Pinning them down and rubbing dirt in their faces; even making them eat it." Bren felt his heart rate increasing again, spurred on by bad memories – by the sting of wounds still rawer than he'd realized.

"And no one told the teachers?"

Bren shook his head. "No way. Shaun always says he'll make life miserable for anyone who grasses on him. So everyone kept their mouths shut, and after a while he left them alone. Except me. He thought I'd told everyone what I saw. Kept giving me a hard time." He let out a tired groan. "I was starting to hope he'd moved on. But after what happened yesterday, at school after English and..."

"And what?"

Bren's mouth was open but – remembering Shaun's warning – he couldn't bring himself to talk about Shaun's shaming by the tower.

Cary tutted. "Shaun was just trying to save face, you know. Yesterday, when he hassled you by the lockers."

Bren's eyes met Cary's. "And whose fault d'you think that is?"

Cary pulled back, almost flinching beneath Bren's gaze. "Hey. Honest, Bren. I'm really sorry. I didn't mean to cause trouble. I was just standing up to him. If I'd backed down, he'd have won. In front of everyone. People like Shaun..."

He shook his head bitterly. "They don't deserve the satisfaction."

"Oh yeah? Then—"

"*Sshh!*" Cary clutched Bren's arm. His eyes were wide and he had a finger pushed to his lips. "*They're coming...*"

Cary was right. Bren heard footsteps drawing closer, grinding through snow. Someone hacked up phlegm and spat it away. Bren heard the sticky wad hit the ice; they were *that* close, separated from him by just the brick wall. And then Shaun's voice – a seething snarl.

"...run all they want, but they've got to go to school. There's no way fake-ginge is wriggling out of this."

"Or Bren." Alex's voice.

At the mention of his name, Bren couldn't help ducking low, even though he was already hidden.

"*Especially* Bren," grunted Shaun. "What's *he* think he's doing? Beakface is forgetting his place. There's no way he's gonna try that crap again. Not after I'm done with him."

A cackle from Isaiah. "Funny though, isn't it? Beakface to the rescue."

"Yeah," grunted Alex. "Watch out for beakface! He'll sneeze you away with his massive schnoz!"

"Hurricane coming!" hooted Isaiah.

Shaun didn't sound amused. "He won't be able to sneeze when I've rearranged his nose."

"You'd do him a favour! His nose is so big he can smell

the future!" Bren heard scuffs and cackles, as if Isaiah and Alex were hopping about like excited dogs.

Bren listened closely – with his eyes clenched shut – while their footsteps faded. When the voices were gone, he opened his eyes and croaked beneath his breath, "I'm *so* dead."

He waited a little longer, until Cary got up and cautiously mounted the wall. Bren watched him climb. "You think it's safe to go out there?"

Cary was peeking over the wall's top, with his face towards the Dale. "Yeah. They're gone."

"You sure?"

"Yup."

Bren followed, and they both dropped to the path before heading warily up Bradbury Avenue. Cary tapped Bren's arm. "Hey, you wanna hang out? Safety in numbers, right?"

Bren shook his head. "Got to get home." His thoughts were already on Furthermoor. And Cary had stirred enough trouble as it was.

"Suit yourself." Cary shrugged, then grimaced at the footprints in the snow. "Did you hear those two, though? Sucking up to Shaun like he's god's gift?" Much of the fear had left Cary's voice; he sounded more disgusted than scared. "Makes me sick. They don't even like him."

Bren turned his head. "Course they like him."

"Nah. They're just scared of him. People like Shaun don't have friends. Not real ones. Even you've got more friends than he has."

Bren's eyebrows shot up. "'Even me'?"

"Well, I'm just saying...you like to keep to yourself. And, you know..." Cary trailed off, his expression shifting into something different – something more thoughtful. He almost looked glum. "I get that."

Bren stared at Cary, puzzled, until a thought made him stop. "Hang on. Which friends are you saying I *have* got? I mean...compared to Shaun."

Cary stopped too. That look left his face when he cocked his head at Bren, confused but amused. "Well... Me, for a start."

Bren was thrown. A tight warmth rushed to his cheeks, and he thought of Evie and Mum – of all their urging him to see more friends.

He spoke before he could think. "Um, actually... If you still want, maybe we *could* hang out? Like you said, for safety in numbers?" He rubbed the back of his neck. "I mean, you don't have to."

Cary was smiling. "Sure. What do you wanna do? Fancy joining the footie by the tower?"

A swift shake of Bren's head. "No way. Shaun might be there." Even if Shaun wasn't, Bren didn't feel up to a crowd.

"Good point." Cary rubbed his lips, deep in thought. "You could come to mine, if you like. Maybe have a kickabout in the garden?"

"Where do you live?"

"Carroll Crescent."

Bren knew Carroll Crescent. It was on the edge of the estate, with bigger houses than the rest of Williamsborough. "Okay. I'll just tell my dad." He got his phone out, texting with numb fingers to say he'd be home in time for dinner.

"Cool."

Bren put his phone away. When they carried on walking, he lowered his voice.

"I do have friends, by the way." He put a hand to his trouser pocket, felt Evie's watch through the fabric. "Just because you haven't seen them, it doesn't mean they're not...real." The final word broke in his throat, and he sucked in a shaky breath before looking away.

"Real?" echoed Cary. "You mean as in...genuine?"

Bren nodded, with his eyes to the ground. "Yeah. Genuine."

Chapter Twelve

Bark and Bite

As they trekked through Williamsborough, Bren couldn't stop glancing occasionally over his shoulder. It didn't escape his notice that Cary was doing the same.

They soon reached a semi-detached on Carroll Crescent. Cary slid a key into the door. "Come on in," he said. "You'll have to take your shoes off – carry them through to the garden."

Bren peered past him into the hallway. It had been so long since he'd visited someone else's home. "Sure."

Cary ushered him in. As they toed off their school shoes, Cary slammed the front door and a voice called from upstairs.

"That you, Cary?"

Cary yelled back up the staircase. "Yeah, Dad! I've brought a friend over! Gonna kick the ball about in the garden!"

"I'll be down in a mo!" Cary's dad's voice wobbled with echo; he must have been in the bathroom. "In the middle of something!"

"Ew, Dad! Too much detail!"

"Not *that*. I'm fixing the leaky tap."

"Whatever." Cary dropped his backpack and gestured for Bren to do the same.

The hallway was clean, spacious and warm, and Bren felt glad to be out of the cold. He glanced about, taking in plants and ornaments and a bowl full of keys, along with some framed photos on the wall. Most of them were a bit abstract – skylines, brickwork, close-ups of seashells – while others featured Cary and his parents. In one of them, a much younger Cary stood grinning on a stadium seat, with his mum laughing and hugging his waist.

"Which stadium's that?" asked Bren, pointing at the picture.

Cary's eyes rose. "St James' Park."

"You support Newcastle?"

"Yeah. That's where we lived when I first got into football. My mum and dad took me to St James' a lot. We moved to Manchester after that, then Bristol, but I always supported Newcastle."

"Wow. You've really been around."

"Yeah."

Again, Bren saw that look – wistful and serious – flicker

across Cary's face. Bren was still doing his best to hide how shaken Bradbury Avenue had left him; perhaps Cary was doing the same.

"It's cos of my mum's work," Cary went on – cheery again, though something creased the edges of his eyes. Carrying his shoes, he led Bren from the hallway to the kitchen. "She's an engineer. Works in construction. Sometimes she has to go where the best projects are."

"That's cool." Bren meant it. He was thinking of Evie, knowing she'd approve. "Do you mind it, though? I mean, moving so much?" His eyes roamed the kitchen as he spoke, and he noticed a Chinese calendar by the window, red and gold with cute, cartoonish animals.

Cary shrugged. "It's not always great, I guess. But I prefer it to Mum always being away."

"What's your dad do?"

"He's a photographer. Business events. Weddings. Stuff like that. He prefers taking arty photos, though."

"Like the ones in the corridor?"

"Yeah, those are his."

"They're really good."

Cary gave a deep, warm smile that had Bren smiling too. "Thanks, bud. I'll tell him you said that. He'll really appreciate it."

They slipped their shoes on and entered the cold again, passing through some patio doors into the garden. Cary sprinted ahead across snow-covered grass, then kicked a ball towards Bren. It almost caught Bren by surprise, but he managed to hop to one side and punt it back.

"Thanks, by the way," said Cary. "For helping me out earlier." He sent the ball back to Bren.

"Right. Yeah." Bren frowned at the ball beneath his foot, his mood sinking at the thought of Shaun.

"You were pretty awesome," Cary went on. "Sending Shaun and the other two down the alley like that, then knowing where to hide. That was really smart."

"Smart?" echoed Bren, still frowning.

"Yeah. What you did was dead brave."

Bren lifted his eyes. "I'm not brave."

"Could have fooled me, bud. Not many people would've done what you did. I'm not sure I would have. You've got guts."

Bren almost laughed at that, but the sincerity in Cary's expression stopped him.

"I mean it," said Cary. "I don't know why you're pulling that face." He scratched his forehead. "I also don't know why Shaun keeps going on about your nose. It's hardly massive, is it? Some people just look for stuff to pick on." He pretended to pick his nose. "No pun intended."

Bren couldn't help smiling. They chuckled together – a giddy mix of nerves and relief – and passed the ball back and forth. Bren was soon flicking the ball into the air and trying some tricks. He was rusty, but better than he'd expected. It felt so good to handle a football again. He bounced it off his knee and kicked it to Cary.

"You've got skills!" Cary headed it back but it went wide, soaring towards a tree by the garden fence.

"Thanks! I—" A rasping caw stole Bren's words. Freezing on the spot, his eyes followed the sound, and he saw a crow perched on a branch above the ball.

Cary's voice from behind. "What's up?"

Bren's eyes wouldn't leave the crow. It returned his gaze, watching him coolly with black, unblinking eyes.

Cary came close, looking back and forth between Bren and the bird. "You've got a problem with that crow?"

The muscles in Bren's neck and shoulders had clamped up. "No," he began, his voice hoarse and slow. "It's got a problem with me. The crows round here... Lately they've started...attacking me."

"Serious?" Cary began to grin, though his smile quickly became a frown. "Wait, you really mean it?"

Stepping closer to the crow, Cary began jumping up and down, waving his arms and hollering. "Shoo! Shoo!" With a ruffle of feathers, the crow screeched and took to the air – over the fence and out of sight.

Cary faced Bren, smiling again. "Did you hurt one of their babies or something?"

"Babies?"

"I saw a thing on Newsround once. There was this guy in India who accidentally knocked a baby crow out of a tree. He was attacked by crows for ages after that. They waited outside his house and everything."

Bren's chin dropped. "Really?"

"Really. Crows are *super* smart. They remember the faces of human threats. And they make tools and have funerals and all sorts. Amazing, really."

Bren eyed the sky. "That might be it. I tried to get a bird off the road yesterday. It was small – might've been a young crow. But I dropped it by accident. That's when they started attacking me. It was...horrible." Bren paused, wondering again if the attack had something to do with Featherly turning up in Furthermoor. His gaze drifted to Cary. "What happened to that Indian guy? Did he get the crows to stop?"

"I think it just kind of wore off, after a while."

Bren's eyes were back on the tree.

"Don't worry." Cary punched his arm. "Next time a crow gives you the evil eye, do what I did just now. Psych it out. It's just like Shaun and his type. You've got to handle them the same way."

Bren cocked his head. "The same way?"

"Sure. Don't let them know you're scared. Look them right in the eye." Cary flicked his fringe from his forehead. "Bullies are like animals – like that crow I just scared off.

They can smell your fear; it makes them feel tough. So hide it. Do what I do. Puff yourself up and make some noise. Make your bark worse than your bite. It puts bullies off. They usually go looking for easier prey."

Bren made a bitter noise. "Easier prey like me, you mean?"

Cary bit his lip, his forehead creasing.

Bren sucked in some icy air. "Anyway, they don't always leave you alone, do they?"

"Hm?"

"Shaun didn't leave *you* alone. Look what happened today."

Cary's mouth tightened. "Shaun needs more work. I'll step things up a gear. But remember – he's a wuss. All bullies are."

Bren scoffed.

"I'm serious! You ever seen Shaun pick on anyone bigger than him? Or even the same size?"

After giving this some thought, Bren shook his head.

"Well there you go. He's a wimp. Bullies always are – and that's what really winds me up about them. That's why I couldn't stand seeing Shaun laying into you. It takes a real coward to push someone smaller around." Cary nodded soberly to himself. "Trust me, Shaun's a wuss. He'll leave you alone if you bark back."

"What if I'm...too scared to bark back?"

"It's just like I said. Hide your fear. Fake it till you make it."

Bren was staring at the tree again. Cary made it sound so easy, but it wasn't at all.

When they both fell silent, Bren noticed how dark it was – how cold his hands and toes were. The light from the windows spilled across dark, bluish snow.

He turned his face slowly to Cary, clearing his throat. He wanted to ask something, but it took some effort to force the words. "Cary?"

"Yeah?"

"Why do you keep...like...being so friendly to me?"

Cary frowned, as if trying to understand the question. "Why wouldn't I?"

"Cos you're Cary." Bren gave a gloomy shrug. "You're Mr Popular. You're even hanging out with the girls in Year Nine. And I'm just..." He gestured from his duffel coat to his shoes. "I'm just...me." He felt his cheeks burn and had to look away.

When Cary didn't respond, Bren began to feel sick in the cold. He should have kept his mouth shut.

But then Cary spoke. "I've not always been liked, you know."

Bren huffed and kicked some snow. "Yeah, right."

"I'm serious. I told you about all the times I changed schools, yeah?"

Bren's eyes were still on the ground, but he nodded.

"Well," continued Cary, "the first time I changed schools – when I moved to Manchester – I missed my friends in Newcastle *so* much. Honest, you wouldn't believe it. I was gutted. I missed them so badly I couldn't make friends in my new school. I mean, I didn't even want to. It felt like I'd be abandoning my old ones. I wished so hard to be back in Newcastle. And…looking back now, I think all that moping – all that being alone – helped attract the first bullies I got hassle from. Like I said, they smell that sort of stuff."

Cary sighed, toeing the snow with his shoe. "I learned, though, in the end. After a few months of being lonely and miserable, I started coming out of my shell and made new friends. And it felt great, yeah? That's why I know, now – why I throw myself into new friendships. But before all that, I was a complete loner. By choice. I didn't want to be around people. I didn't want to be surrounded by kids who were happy. I felt like…like I'd lost so much."

Bren had been slowly raising his eyes from the snow. He saw Cary, watching him intently.

"And you know what?" said Cary. "I don't know why, but I sort of see it in you. It reminds me of me back then."

"See what?" mumbled Bren.

"Being so…sad." Cary shrugged. "Like you've lost something too."

Bren's knees almost buckled beneath him. He swallowed painfully, his face darting to one side.

For a fleeting moment, he felt an urge to tell Cary about Evie – about how she'd died on the Dale just ten months ago. About how he'd lost the sister who meant more to him than he'd even realized. But then Bren thought of the way his friends had started acting around him, and he bit his tongue. He liked Cary. He didn't want to ruin this.

"You okay?" asked Cary. "I didn't mean to—"

"Hey guys!" A call from the patio. Bren turned and saw Cary's dad waving from the door. He had Cary's warm smile, along with a damp rag draped over the shoulder of his cardigan. "Who's your friend, Cary?"

Friend. The word took some of the cold from Bren's fingers.

"This is Bren," Cary called back. "Bren, this is my dad."

Cary's dad gave a little wave. "Nice to meet you, Bren."

Bren forced a smile. "You too."

"You staying for dinner? We're having pork chops – Cary's favourite."

Bren fumbled with his phone to check the time. It was nearly six o'clock. "Sorry, I have to get home. My dinner'll be waiting for me."

"No worries. Another time, eh?" Cary's dad turned his gaze to his son. "How was school?"

Cary screwed up his face, suddenly serious. "Actually,

yeah… Today something happened. I…" He faltered when Bren nudged his back. As he glanced across, Bren gave a discreet shake of the head, begging with his eyes for Cary not to go on.

"Sorry?" asked Cary's dad.

"It's…nothing." Cary forced a shrug. "I'll tell you later."

"Okay. I'd better get to those chops. Mum'll be back soon. Hopefully we'll see you around, Bren." With another smile, Cary's dad whipped the cloth from his shoulder and disappeared into the kitchen, closing the patio door behind him.

Cary shot a look at Bren. "What's wrong? I was gonna tell him what Shaun did."

Bren's face had turned pale. "You can't tell your parents."

"Course I can. I need my phone back."

"But your parents… They might tell the teachers."

"Exactly. That's what I meant by stepping things up with Shaun."

A surge of queasiness hit Bren's gut. "You can't tell the teachers."

"Why not? Because Shaun'll take it out on me? He'd only get into more trouble."

"It's not just that."

"Then what is it?"

Clutching his churning stomach, Bren took a deep breath. "Well, it's… It's grassing. It's not…cool."

Cary shook his head. "I'll tell you what's not cool: people like Shaun getting away with this crap cos everyone's too scared to do something about it."

"But there's...I don't know...like a school code. You don't snitch on people."

"Why not?"

"You just don't. It's...embarrassing, you know?"

"The only person who should be embarrassed is Shaun."

"*Please*," begged Bren. "Don't tell your parents."

"But Shaun's got my *phone*, Bren."

"I'll help you get it back. I promise. We'll figure something out. But let's do it ourselves, okay? I don't want any parents or teachers on Shaun's back. It'll only make things worse."

Cary grimaced, lifting his palms in exasperation.

"I've got to go," said Bren. "I told my dad I'd be back by now."

With Cary plodding behind him, Bren crossed the patio, entered the house, took off his shoes and carried them to the front door. After saying a polite goodbye to Mr Yue, he grabbed his backpack, whispered a terse "*please*" to Cary, then started jogging home.

Chapter Thirteen

The Snap

As he reached the house, Bren saw his dad peering anxiously from behind the living-room curtain. The front door opened before he could even get his key out.

"Bren! Where have you been?" The creases around Dad's eyes looked deep. His greying hair was even scruffier than usual. He stepped aside, letting Bren in.

"Relax, Dad. I'm hardly late. I was just…hanging out."

"Hanging out?"

Bren took off his shoes and peeled away his cold, soggy socks. "Yeah, hanging out." He shrugged. "With a friend."

Dad's head jerked back on his neck. "A friend?"

"Yeah, a friend." Bren hung up his coat. "Why d'you sound so surprised?"

Dad's lips fluttered before he replied. "Um, no. Not surprised."

Bren saw his dad's shoulders drop, losing some of their

tautness. A faint smile began to creep onto his face. The skin by his eyes creased again, but in a warmer way. "That's fine, Bren. It's...great. But you should have told me exactly where you were. I was worried."

"Sorry, Dad. I will next time." Bren lowered his eyes and made for the stairs.

"Where're you going? Your dinner's waiting."

"You eat, Dad. I'll eat later. I snacked at my friend's." Bren took the steps two at a time. He was desperate for his room. He'd never been keener to see Evie.

"Oh. Okay. Um, Mum'll be back late tonight."

"Yeah, I know. Work."

"Bren?"

"Yeah?"

"Could you...hang on a minute?"

Bren paused at the top of the stairs. He closed his eyes, took a deep breath and turned around. "What?"

"Mum was in touch earlier. She got a call. From school."

Bren took a step back down the staircase. "From school?"

"Your head teacher called. She told Mum they're a bit... concerned about your school work."

Mr Okorafor. He must have spoken to Mrs Sendak. While groaning to himself, Bren noticed the way Dad was kneading his fingers. He was enjoying this exchange even less than Bren.

"Well..." Dad couldn't seem to look at Bren while he spoke. Instead, he focused on a patch of carpet by his son's feet. "They said you're not finishing your work. They're worried you're having problems focusing." He frowned and swallowed. "Maybe cos of—"

"Can we talk about this later, Dad?" Bren sucked in his lips. "I'm really... I need the loo. Like, really badly."

Dad actually looked relieved. "Um... Sure. Okay. We'll talk about it when...when Mum's back. Sure." His eyes darted to Bren's face. "You okay?"

"Will be when I get on the toilet."

Dad was already retreating from the staircase. "Good. Yeah, good. Come down whenever you're hungry. There's cottage pie waiting."

Bren spun on the stairs, jogged the rest of the way and slammed his bedroom door behind him.

Tick.

Tock.

Tick.

Tock.

Bren was so glad to feel Furthermoor's sunshine on his neck. He savoured its heat while he descended, climbing past branches laden with gears, increasing his distance from the wardrobe's gloom above.

The sun warmed his bare feet, and when he looked down he saw Evie waiting below, stood with her arms crossed in the rippling meadow. Her grim expression twisted his stomach into knots.

"Hey, big sis."

"Hey, little bro. Glad you're here."

Bren dropped to the ground. "What's wrong?"

"I'll show you."

Using the watch, Bren cleared a path through brittle blooms. And when they reached the forest's edge, he saw the problem.

"Not again," he muttered, entering the shade and crouching by a faun. The creature lay on its side, its gemstone eyes twitching and dull. One of its rear legs kicked and whirred, kicked and whirred, while exposed gears lurched within its bared metal innards.

Bren shook his head at the gash in the faun's belly – at the torn felt and twisted wire frame. "Featherly."

Evie nodded.

Bren took out his watch and started flicking cogs. Springs and sprockets lay pooled by the creature's open stomach; as Bren tweaked the watch they began to move, rolling past felt to find their places inside the faun.

The faun was soon fixed and prancing away. It sent clockwork finches soaring from the undergrowth, but Bren's eyes were on the branches above. He peered into the canopy, shouting into shadows. "Come out, Featherly! Come say sorry for what you did!"

The woods didn't reply.

Bren huffed beneath his breath. "Who's the coward now?"

Evie tapped his arm. "Bren?"

"Yeah?"

"There's more."

While Evie led the way, Bren told her what had happened that afternoon. But as they continued through the woods, from mangled animal to broken beast, Bren found it increasingly hard to talk. He paused to crouch by each fallen creature. With every repair, his feelings shifted from anger at Featherly to a drained, tired heartache, deep and dark at the core of his chest.

Hares came back to life, twitched their wire whiskers and bolted into bushes. Felted moths flexed their mended wings, rose from Bren's hands and fluttered away. A cockchafer beetle whirled its gears, before ambling into the air and perching on ivy.

On and on it went: a trail of torn animals and silvery ruin. Bren shook his head while they walked, wondering again how this could be happening in Furthermoor.

They were soon by the lake; its turquoise crystal

sparkled between the trees. Bren got to his knees, about to start work on a ferret with ruby eyes. But then, a clumsy rustle from above, before something bony and black dropped from the trees.

Bren didn't look up to acknowledge Featherly's presence, but he could see him at the edge of his vision. A rank, dusty smell seemed to fill Bren's nostrils.

He ground his teeth. His eyes flitted between the ferret and watch. "Why'd you do it?"

"Do what, little fleshling?" came Featherly's rasp.

"Hurt these animals. Rip them apart." Bren lifted his gaze to Featherly, who was squatting nearby and cocking his beaked hood. His gangly arms were pinched between his knees, clasped and rubbing.

Bren felt Evie's hand on his shoulder. He stood up beside her. "The animals here don't have any meat," he said. "You know they don't. But you're still doing –" he pointed at the ferret – "all this. Why?"

Gibbering within his hood, Featherly lowered his beak towards the broken creature. "Passing time," he replied. "Getting an inkling of how things work, here in my whimsied home."

"Just stop it." Bren's voice trembled with emotion. "Leave my things – *Evie's* things – alone."

Featherly belched and chattered. "I've been watching you. While you fix your toys." A nod of his hood towards the green watch. "Seeing how the lord of the land uses his timepiece. An impressive little trinket, yes-yes-yes. All those cogs and combinations, all those tiny tweaks of the realm. And the power to conjure images from the real world… It's quite the marvel."

Bren snapped the watch shut, shoved it into his pocket. "It's none of your business."

A dry cackle. "I've listened, too. Young master's found some pluck."

"What are you talking about?"

"This Cary of yours, rescued from the wolf's lair."

Bren glanced over his shoulder. "How long were you following us?"

"Long enough." Featherly rubbed his grey, twitching fingers. "And didn't it feel *good*, for the meek to be bold? For the lonely to earn a friend?"

Bren's face darkened. "I'm not lonely."

A hoarse, chittering laugh. "But of *course* you are." Featherly's hood snapped towards Evie. "Isn't that so, sister fleshling? You'll admit to your sibling's loneliness, won't you? Even while he fools himself?"

"I…" Evie's mouth formed shapes. "Bren's just…"

Her eyes went to Bren. He could see from her expression that she agreed with Featherly.

Featherly's attention returned to Bren. "Yes-yes-yes, there's reward in aiding the needy. So why not help me, young master of the realm? Why not put blood in your beasts and meat in my belly?"

Bren shook his head. "Never. I'll never feed you. Go back to wherever you came from."

"But I came from *you*. And it seems a little part of you won't let me go. This is none of my doing. Never once did I ask to be here. So be kind, lord of the land. Give a poor imaginary creature meat for his gut."

Featherly clasped his crooked fingers together – a mockery of pleading. The sight of his flaking, filthy fingernails turned Bren's stomach.

He turned to Evie for support, but she didn't seem to share his disgust. If anything, she was watching Featherly with growing curiosity.

She noticed Bren looking at her. Her voice was quiet. A little unsure. "Maybe... Maybe you could give him... something, Bren? Like...just a little—"

"No," snapped Bren. "You're not seriously taking his side, are you?"

Evie tugged awkwardly at her hair. "Course not. Never. It's just that... He's right, in a way. He's not chosen to be here." Bren saw her throat move as she swallowed. "I guess I...know how he feels. I didn't choose to—"

"*Stop.*" Bren pushed his palms against his ears. He scrunched up his eyes, felt a tear run down his cheek.

Then he shook his head, glaring at Featherly. "You're

ruining...*everything*. You're hurting my animals. You're making a mess of Furthermoor. You're calling me a coward and next thing I know I'm sticking my neck out for Cary and now Shaun's going to *kill* me. And on top of that, you're turning my sister against me!"

Evie put a gentle hand on his arm. "Bren, he's not turning—"

But Bren pulled away. He stepped towards Featherly and Featherly stepped towards him. While Bren's chest swelled, Featherly's wings flexed on their scrawny bones.

"Don't take it to heart," cawed Featherly, "if your sister won't do as you please. After all, the poor thing's not even real. She's make-believe and long gone. Buried in soil – a phantom and a ghost."

"No!" The watch was open again in Bren's hands. Lost in rage, he was barely aware of the cogs he twisted in opposite directions. Pulleys began to turn, tautening a cable in the groove by Featherly's feet.

Bren kept twisting. A squeaking groan was heard, getting louder and louder until – with a loud *crack* – the cable snapped. It whipped through the air, barely visible as it lashed the inside of Featherly's hood and sent him reeling.

Bren's rage evaporated. "Oh god," he breathed, his mouth falling open.

Evie gripped his arm. "What did you...?" She was as much in shock as Bren.

Featherly was on his feet again. He ruffled his featherbare wings and pushed a finger into his hood. It came back out smeared with black, sticky blood.

While Bren gaped at that glistening finger, Featherly began to chuckle. His laughter began as a dry, rasping sound, which got louder and louder while he fanned out his wings. "Well. The young master's grown some backbone. The little lord has *claws*."

Bren shook his head. "I…didn't mean to—"

"Do it again," hissed Featherly.

"What?"

"I said, 'Do it again.'"

Bren was backing away. "No. No way."

"Don't shrink away now, young master. Sharpen those claws, show your nerve. It felt good, didn't it?"

Bren took another step back.

"I *know* you, little fleshling. You wanted to hurt me. It felt goooood."

Bren shook his head again, as much to convince himself as anyone else. While he refused to admit it to Featherly, it *had* felt good – just for a furious, fleeting moment. But the feeling had gone as quickly as it came. All that was left now was horror and shame – a self-contempt so fierce it coloured his cheeks and twisted his gut.

Featherly watched him shaking where he stood. He began to tut. "Ever the coward, even with all that power in your hand." He pointed his bloody finger at the watch, shaking his head. "It's *pathetic*."

And with that, Featherly fluttered up into the branches and was gone – just a dark flapping in distant trees.

"Bren," breathed Evie.

Bren hugged himself, trying to calm down. His rapid breaths began to slow. "I'm sorry," he croaked. "I shouldn't have done that. But he… The things he said… They…"

"It's okay," shushed Evie, taking him in her arms. "I know. It must have hurt."

She held her little brother and rocked him gently, until a faint sound pierced the canopy. Bren's name, soaring on the wind.

The siblings peered up as one. "It's Mum," said Evie. "She sounds peeved."

Nodding, Bren adjusted the watch and plodded towards a turning tree. "Yeah, I'd better go."

Tock.

Tick.

Tock.

Tick.

Bren blinked and there was Mum, leaning in through his bedroom doorway. Her face was silhouetted against the light from the landing, but Bren could tell from the lift of her shoulders that she was in a foul mood.

"*Bren*," she snapped. "Are you ignoring me?"

Bren sat up, rubbing his eyes. "No, Mum."

"How many times do I have to call for you?" She shook her head. "This is exactly what Mrs Sendak's talking about. Come downstairs right now. We need to have a talk."

"Okay, Mum."

Mum spun on her heels and thumped down the stairs. Bren groaned and flopped back onto the bed, until a shout from below sent him rushing from his room.

PART FOUR
WEDNESDAY

Chapter Fourteen

Between Worlds

The next day, Bren hovered awkwardly by the door to Mrs Sendak's office. He'd been sent that way by Mrs Burgess, his maths teacher, just after the school bell rang for lunch, and had sidled through the corridors on even higher alert than usual. The last thing he wanted was to bump into Shaun, Isaiah, Alex – or even Cary. He just wanted to be left alone.

While hesitating at the head teacher's door, he heard footsteps from around the corner, so he knocked, timidly but quickly.

"Come in," came Mrs Sendak's voice.

Bren pushed the handle, slipped through and closed the door quietly behind him.

Mrs Sendak looked up and shut the folder on her desk. "Ah, Bren. Thank you for coming."

"'S okay," mumbled Bren, his eyes flitting to the toes of his school shoes.

"Please, take a seat."

Bren shuffled past shelves and cabinets to sit on the chair opposite Mrs Sendak.

"How are you?"

"Good."

"Would you mind looking at me, Bren? There's no need to be so anxious. You're not in trouble."

Bren lifted his eyes. Mrs Sendak, in her dark chequered blazer, was watching him warmly.

Bren cleared his throat. "Is this about…my work?" It needn't be. He'd had his fill about that from Mum last night.

Mrs Sendak's smile widened. "Don't worry, Bren. It's not about that." She flicked her short grey hair. "Though I'm sure you'll start focusing more on your work now, won't you?"

A faint nod.

"Good. You were always a very gifted student. Particularly in art and design. Very imaginative. But no, I've called you in today to talk about Cary. And Shaun."

Bren's neck and shoulders tensed. He felt his breathing change, coming harder now through his nostrils.

"I received a call this morning," continued Mrs Sendak, "from Cary's parents. They told me that yesterday, while Cary was on his way home from school, Shaun, Alex and Isaiah stole his phone and trapped him in an abandoned house."

Bren's gaze sank to his lap. He could feel Mrs Sendak watching him, waiting for a response. But he said nothing.

She cleared her throat. "As I hope you know, Bren, we take such things very seriously here at Williamsborough Academy. But it's difficult to act, unfortunately. Shaun, Alex and Isaiah completely deny any knowledge of these events. Each of them claims that Cary's making this up to get them into trouble – though they can't imagine why. So, this has become a tricky matter to navigate. It's Cary's word against theirs."

Mrs Sendak fell silent again. Bren kept his gaze low, rubbed the tightening tendons behind his neck. He had an inkling of where this was going.

His head teacher drummed her fingers on the desk. "But you might be able to help clear this up, Bren. Cary says you were a witness – that you saw the entire thing. Is this true?"

Bren couldn't reply. His head was buzzing with thoughts, muddled by panic.

Mrs Sendak's voice again. "Bren? Is it true?"

Bren's hand drifted towards the watch in his pocket, but he caught himself and pushed it against his thigh. He wished so hard to be away from here – to escape to Furthermoor.

"Bren," repeated Mrs Sendak, a little firmer now. "Is this what your teachers are talking about? You seem to be drifting off." Her tone softened again. "Please, answer the question. I shouldn't need to say that there'll be implications for Cary if we discover he's making false accusations. Especially when they're so serious."

Gradually, Bren lifted his face. He spoke slowly, forcing himself to push out each word. "If I say something, will Shaun and the others find out?"

Mrs Sendak shook her head. "Everything you say will be completely confidential."

Bren nodded and lowered his eyes once more. If he didn't tell the truth, Cary would get into trouble. And he wouldn't be believed if Shaun did anything else to him – which Bren had no doubt he would.

Sighing through his nostrils, Bren sucked his upper lip. Cary had complicated everything, for sure. But he'd also stood up for him. He'd been kind. He was his friend. He didn't deserve to get into trouble.

Without lifting his head, Bren glanced at Mrs Sendak. His words came in a mumble. "'S true."

Again, Bren could sense her watching him. He shrugged. He had nothing more to say.

Mrs Sendak finally spoke. "Thank you, Bren. I realize that can't have been easy for you." She drummed her fingernails against the desk again.

At the edge of his vision, Bren saw her leaning forward. Her tone was tender. "In fact, you seem worried.

I'm…familiar with that look. So I feel I should ask… Bren?"

Bren heard the genuine concern in Mrs Sendak's voice. He couldn't help raising his face.

The skin around her lips creased with an uneasy smile. "Do you have any reason to be frightened of Shaun? Has he given…*you* any trouble? Not just yesterday. I mean, at any time at all?"

Bren stared at her. His mouth went dry and his throat began to swell. His lips shifted, very slightly, unsure of what sounds to form.

And then, finally, he replied.

"No. Never."

His lie came as much from embarrassment as it did from fear of Shaun. There was no way he could admit to it – to being pushed around for months now, like some cowering, skulking wimp. Like a pathetic coward, just as Featherly had said.

Bren felt the shame pressing against his lips, as cold and heavy as a padlock.

Mrs Sendak's smile stayed put, though her forehead furrowed. "Okay, Bren. But I certainly hope that, were you ever to get trouble from Shaun – or any other students for that matter, online or off, on school grounds or elsewhere – you'd tell us. We take bullying very seriously at Williamsborough Academy."

It took all Bren's strength to keep his face raised to his head teacher. "Thank you, Mrs Sendak. I'll remember that."

Mrs Sendak looked at him for several seconds, then pulled back to rest against her office chair. "Okay. You can go now. Thank you for your help in this matter, Bren. I really appreciate it, and I know Cary and his parents will too."

Bren got up. "What'll happen to Shaun?"

"That's a matter for discussion. But don't worry. Everything will be treated with complete confidentiality." Mrs Sendak nodded once at Bren. "Shaun will never even know that we spoke today."

"Thank you, Mrs Sendak."

Opening the door, Bren peered left and right along the corridor. No one was around, so he took a deep breath and left the office.

It was still lunchtime. Peering across the playground from the school's entrance, Bren saw with great relief that Shaun, Alex and Isaiah weren't loitering by the bike shelter. That made it safer to head for the arts block.

He spotted Cary in the distance, perched on the concrete ping pong table, showing off some sort of dance move and making other pupils laugh. Bren thought for a moment about going to him – about asking him why he'd gone ahead and told his parents. But there were so many people around. And what if Shaun and his lackeys turned up? It was too risky.

Cary looked pretty engrossed in his moves, so Bren made a dash for it. Leaving the doorway, he slipped his hands into his duffel coat, pushed up his shoulders and lowered his head. Then he scurried through the snow piled along the playground's edge – much of it now crushed and hardened into ice – moving briskly but not so fast as to draw attention. Passing the lunchtime football match, he was now almost out of Cary's line of sight, nearing the trees that lined the path to the arts block.

Bren slowed at the thought of those bare, black trees. He didn't look up but heard a caw that sent a shudder down his spine. After faltering, he gritted his teeth and pushed on, lifting his hood to hide his face. Dark wings beat above him, sending lumps of snow falling from branches. Bren's breathing quickened. His legs pumped harder beneath him.

Once safely in the arts block, Bren kept up his pace, opened his backpack and shoved the sandwich and apple from his packed lunch into his face. Time was short; he'd spent too much of the lunch break in Mrs Sendak's office.

Barging into the empty music room, Bren took his place on the carpet behind the drum kit, fumbling in his pocket to find his watch. But when he pulled it out, he looked at its green face and froze.

What if Featherly was waiting for him?

Bren closed his eyes, thinking back to their last encounter – to the things Featherly had said, to what he'd done in return. To clockwork hares and badgers, sprawled on wool-moss with their innards scattered; to bullfinches and kestrels, with feathers plucked and wire frames bare. To the anger and hurt; to the cable that drew blood.

Shaking his head, Bren returned the watch to his pocket. He didn't have the strength. Not today.

He gazed at the door he'd just come through. Beyond it waited the noise and loneliness of the playground. Cary too, and maybe even Shaun. There was no way he could go back out there.

So Bren hugged himself and stayed where he was: sitting on the carpet, trapped between worlds.

Chapter Fifteen

Repeat

That afternoon, after the day's final bell, Bren hurried furtively along the Dale. He didn't slow to watch the kids hanging out by the shops, or to gaze at Ballard Tower in the distance. And he didn't cast a glance down Bradbury Avenue. He just watched his feet and kept walking – each step through the snow a step closer to the safety of his room – and turned gratefully onto Herbert Road. His stomach rumbled as he approached his house; a day of nerves and cold weather had left him hungry.

Reaching for his key, Bren sighed thankfully beneath his hood. He'd somehow got through the day without running into Shaun. He allowed himself a weak smile. That wasn't bad going. He'd been braced for worse.

But then someone hissed his name.

Bren followed the sound. His heart missed a beat when he saw Shaun, leaning out from the corner at the end of the terrace, beckoning with his hand.

Bren slowed to a stop. He raised the key towards the door, his eyes never leaving Shaun.

"*Please*," said Shaun. "Just come over here."

Bren was confused. Shaun looked different. His blue eyes had lost their usual coldness. They were softer, sadder. Bren realized he was pleading.

"Please, Bren. I promise I won't touch you. Never again. I just need to talk. Okay?"

Bren's balled-up hand hovered just centimetres from the door.

"Come *on*, Bren," begged Shaun. His ears jutted, red and cold, from the stubbly sides of his head.

Lowering his hand, Bren tried to force some courage into his voice. "What do you want?"

"I just wanna say sorry."

"Sorry?" Bren didn't believe it. He raised the key again, but when he saw Shaun's pupils flit along the road – as if to check no one was watching – he knew he shouldn't have lingered. The crunch of footsteps came from behind, and a hand clasped Bren's mouth before he could even yell.

It was Alex and Isaiah. With Bren's cries still smothered, they dragged him to the corner where Shaun was waiting. All three of them grabbed his limbs, and alleys and gardens tumbled by as they lugged him through gaps in fences and bushes.

Bren thrashed and struggled, but the three of them were too strong. While Alex checked round the corner of another terrace, they pulled up their puffer jacket hoods. "It's clear," hissed Alex, and they were soon dragging Bren across a snowy road.

Bren's eyes darted feverishly to and fro. He saw metal gratings and satellite dishes. An overturned trolley.

Bradbury Avenue.

Bren thrashed all the harder, kicking his legs and screaming into Shaun's hand. Isaiah and Alex sniggered at his efforts. Before Bren knew it, they were in another alley.

They yanked him through the junkyard garden and kitchen door. While they carried him over tiles and litter, Shaun leered and grunted. "I got in trouble for yesterday, beakface. Got a right telling off from Mrs Sendak."

Musty darkness and peeling walls – the hallway. "I wouldn't give a crap about that," Shaun went on, "but she called my dad."

Dirty floorboards fell away below Bren; he was being hauled up the stairs. His stomach churned and twisted. He felt an urge to throw up, but could only gag on the spit that pooled in his mouth.

Though he couldn't see Shaun's face in the darkness, he heard the sneer in his voice. "There's one thing I didn't get, though. Why'd they believe Cary and not us? It was three against one. Someone must have snitched." He huffed and spat. "Are you a snitch, ginger nut? Wouldn't be the *first* time, would it?"

Bren shook his head, but his cries of denial were smothered by Shaun's palm. Suddenly his feet hit the floor and his mouth was free. The word on his lips became a yelp as he was shoved through a doorway.

He twisted to see the door slam shut, heard the key rattle until it turned with a clunk.

Shaun's voice through the keyhole: "Whether you snitched or not, you shouldn't have stuck your big freckled nose in. What happened yesterday was between me and Cary."

Bren swayed and pivoted in the gloom, taking in the mattress propped against the wall, the metal grating on the window.

"What're you playing at?" spat Shaun. "First you're helping that cocky little fake-ginge, then you're grassing me up to the teachers! Who'd you think you are, big man?"

A chorus of cackles. Isaiah and Alex.

"It's hilaaaarious," scoffed Shaun. "You think you're some sort of tough guy now? You seriously trying to grow a pair?"

Bren stared at the door, too afraid to guess what answer Shaun wanted to hear.

"Don't worry," grunted Shaun. "You can have some quality time in the thinking room. I'm gonna make sure you never mess up again. So repeat after me." He spoke slowly in a slurred voice. "My name's Bren."

Bren's lips moved, croaking the words.

"I can't heeeear you, beakface!"

Bren stepped to the door, his voice cracking into a shout. "My name's Bren!"

"And I'm a snivelling little grass!"

"I'm a snivelling little grass."

"And a whiny no-mates loser!"

"A whiny no-mates loser."

"Cos my sister got hit by a car, boo hoo hoo."

"Cos my...my sister..." The words caught in Bren's throat, sharp and jagged enough to bring tears to his eyes.

Shaun shouted over hyena hoots and cackles. "And I'll never snitch again!"

"I'll...I'll never snitch again!"

Shaun stopped then, and the laughter died away. The door banged and shuddered, thumped by the kick of a boot.

"You know what?" Shaun's voice was slick with disgust. "It's pathetic. You're embarrassing. This isn't even fun. You're more annoying now than when you were trying to show some guts."

Bren stepped closer to the door, scared to respond in case he said the wrong thing. Someone hacked up phlegm and spat it out. There was a click from the keyhole as the door was unlocked. "Let yourself out when you've learned your lesson, beakface. And don't you *dare* grass on me again, or this is just the beginning."

Bren hugged himself and shivered, listening to every laugh while the trio thundered downstairs and out of the house. Then he waited for several minutes, keen to make sure they were long gone before he left the room.

All was soon silent. After letting out a hushed, trembling breath, Bren shuffled forward to try the door. But as much as he turned the handle and heaved, the door wouldn't move.

Bren took off his woolly gloves, threw them to the floor and tried again, yanking with both hands. But still the door wouldn't budge.

He gripped harder, pulling and jerking with all his strength.

Nothing. Not even a hint of movement.

"No no no," moaned Bren, getting to his knees, peering into the keyhole's darkness. He remembered how the key had resisted when he'd freed Cary from this room. His throat began to tighten with panic. The lock must have jammed.

Bren tried taking some deep breaths to settle his nerves, but they just came out in tight, panicky bursts. He gripped the door handle again, yanking frantically now, begging with each pull. When nothing happened he started kicking the door, again and again, harder and harder. But the door was too thick, its frame too strong.

Bren's foot began to hurt. He pulled out his phone, and his eyes widened with horror when he tried to unlock it. The screen stayed blank. He held down the on button, but the screen didn't even flicker. His phone was dead. He should have charged it last night.

Bren searched the room, eyeing the filthy carpet and frosty walls; the peeling radiator and grubby mattress; the boarded window with its pricks of light. He banged the windowpane with his fists and knuckles, crying out for help, hammering with his elbows, then returned to the door. He rattled its handle again, kicked and thumped its wood before spinning on the spot, searching for anything he might have missed.

Another trip to the window, knocking and shouting until his voice broke. His elbows began to bruise so he went back to using his fists, wincing as the skin on his knuckles broke and bled. He was soon back at the door, pulling and pleading, kicking and hammering. But none of it was any use.

And that's how it happened. That's how the trouble started with Cary and brought Bren here – trapped and hungry and freezing to death in the thinking room.

That's how Bren ended up huddled on a damp mattress, with the green watch ticking against his ear; with cogs spinning beneath the carpet and a hole unfolding in the floor.

Tick.

Tock.

Tick.

Tock.

Chapter Sixteen

One for Sorrow

Though the sunlight hit Bren as he scrambled down the tree, he barely felt its warmth. He glanced up through the hole in the sky to see the thinking room's ceiling – dim and distant and glimmering with frost – then continued to clamber down, twisting and calling as he went.

"Evie! Evie!"

Movement in the meadow below. A flurry of silk. Clockwork butterflies, lifting off from bluebells.

Evie appeared, her eyes rising to the tree. "Bren?"

"I need you! It's an emergency!" Nearing the ground, Bren jumped down, opened the watch and flicked some cogs.

Evie ran along a path he'd cleared through tall flowers, her green glasses flashing with every step. "What's wrong? What is it?"

Bren jabbed his finger towards the opening above the tree. His words were shrill. "It's Shaun – he's locked me up!

In the same room they put Cary in yesterday!"

"What?" Evie's eyes narrowed and Bren faltered; she looked so much like Mum when she was angry.

He shook his head and pushed his palms against his temples. "They've left but the door's jammed and I can't get out."

"Have you called Mum and Dad?"

"My phone's dead; I can't call anyone. And it's *freezing* in there." He hugged himself at the thought of it. "There's ice on the window and frost on the walls! If I'm stuck in there too long—"

"It could kill you." Evie's hand shot out to grip Bren's wrist. Her hazel eyes flickered up and down his duffel coat. "Bren, it's winter up there. You'll get hypothermia. You need to get out."

Bren nodded fervently. "I *know* that, Evie."

"Have you tried kicking the door?"

"Course I have. It won't move."

"Is there anything you can knock it open with?"

"There's just an old mattress. That's *literally* all there is – the room's completely bare."

"No other doors?"

A shake of the head.

"What about the window? Can you climb out?"

"It's locked and there's metal covering the outside. Bradbury Avenue."

"Maybe you can smash the glass. Even if you can't get past the grating, you can call out for help."

"I tried that. The window won't break." He showed her his torn knuckles. Smeared blood filled the creases between his fingers.

Evie's hand went to her mouth. "This is bad."

"*Really* bad."

"There's got to be a way, though. There's *always* a way."

Evie turned and tapped her lips, scanning the distant woods while she thought. "Have you got your school bag with you?"

"Yeah."

"What's the toughest, hardest thing in there?"

"I guess...my lunch box?"

"You could use that to smash the window."

"That glass is thick, Evie. I doubt it'll work." He glanced at his stinging knuckles. "I'll try, though. You got a plan B?"

Evie's eyes were still on the forest. She turned abruptly to Bren. "Ice."

"Ice?"

"D'you remember that time Dad couldn't get the car doors open?"

"I...don't think so."

"Sure you do. We were heading out to buy a Christmas tree. Dad accidentally snapped the one in the loft."

Memories began to stir. "Oh yeah, the car… Its locks were frozen. From the cold."

Evie grabbed his arm. "*Exactly*. I bet that's what's happened to the lock in that room. You need to defrost it. Loosen it up."

"But Dad used de-icing spray. I don't carry that sort of stuff around in my school bag, Evie."

"There must be some other way to warm it up."

Bren gave this some thought. "Maybe…my breath?"

Evie broke into a grin. "Yes! Breathe into the keyhole. Loosen up the mechanism."

Bren's forehead creased with doubt. "You think that'll work?"

"That or smashing the window with your lunch box. You've got better odds there than you have sitting around freezing to death."

Bren frowned at his sister, until the hope in her eyes had him nodding too. He began to smile. "Okay. You're right. I'd better get back."

He craned his neck towards the opening above the tree, and was about to pocket his watch when some nearby foxgloves twinkled. Something dark shot out from the nodding flowers, knocking Bren's hand as it flew by.

"Wha—" began Bren. His watch soared in an arc through the air, before something leaped with a flap of bony wings and caught it in both hands.

"Featherly!" gasped Evie.

Featherly was still on the move, though he'd turned to jog backwards along an older path, with his hood – still shadowy in the sun-soaked meadow – aimed at Bren and Evie.

"Yes-yes-yessss!" he gibbered. "Featherly and his shiny toy! Featherly, lord of Furthermoor!"

Bren broke into a run the moment Featherly opened the watch. "No!" he shouted, but Featherly's grey fingers were already meddling. The sky dimmed to purple dusk, brightened to scorching blue, dimmed again, brightened again.

"Leave that alone!" cried Bren.

Featherly cawed and cackled, twisting and toying with silver cogs and wheels. Pulleys spun in the undergrowth. Flowers flattened themselves in random directions, as if invisible creatures were bolting through the meadow.

Featherly kept probing and flicking, and gibbered in delight when a grinding noise rose behind Bren.

"Bren!" shouted Evie. "The tree!"

Bren spun on his feet and stopped. The tree was revolving and lowering, corkscrewing back into the ground. Bren squinted past its sinking tip, saw the opening to the real world shrinking in the sky. His racing heart began to pummel his ribs.

"Featherly!" The cry flew from Bren's throat – a shrill

blend of pleading and rage. He turned again, saw the distance growing sickeningly between them. Featherly was at the forest's border now, facing the woods. With a flap of those scabby wings, he leaped into the nearest tree and was lost to shadows.

Bren had to stop and put his palms against his thighs. His lungs throbbed and ached. A wave of coldness had him shivering, even in Furthermoor's sunlight.

Evie skidded to a stop by his side, grabbed both his arms and pulled him upright. "Bren, the opening to that room... It's gone!"

Bren looked miserably at the unbroken sky. Evie was right.

"Can you open it again?" Evie's grip tightened on his arms. "Can you get back?"

Bren shook his head. "I don't have the watch."

Evie followed Bren's gaze to where the hole once was. "But you don't really need it to get back, do you? Can't you just...*will* the hole back? Or just...imagine yourself out of here?"

"I've...I've never tried. I wouldn't know where to start."

"Start here, Bren!"

Bren screwed his eyes shut, trying to visualize the hole returning to the sky. But when he opened his eyes the sky was untouched. He screwed his eyes shut again, this time willing himself back into the thinking room, envisioning himself stirring on its mattress. But again, when he opened his eyes, nothing had changed.

"I can't do it." Bren stared at his sister, who was gaping back with her mouth wide open. "It's like Featherly said. Imagination can't be tamed. It doesn't always do what it's told. Furthermoor has its own *rules*, Evie."

Evie looked wordlessly at Bren for several moments. Gradually the fear left her face, leaving in its place a grimace more obstinate than worried. "Then we have to get the watch from Featherly. It's the only way to get you back to that room before –" a flash of that fear returned, fluttering across her features – "before you know what."

Before Bren could reply, Evie sprinted away through the meadow. Her bare feet pounded the ground beneath her summer dress. Bren followed just behind, but they both faltered when they hit the woods.

Bren scanned the crystal canopy. "How do we find him?"

"We follow his trail."

"Trail?"

"Look." Evie pointed at the remains of a fox, lying next to a pile of stuffing, levers and gears.

Evie rushed past the fox towards a badger, which lay with its face torn to reveal a tin skull. While Bren crouched beside the fox, Evie moved on to a snake draped over a branch. Its eyes and scales were scattered across the ground.

Bren ached to have the watch back in his hand. "I can't even fix them!" It was like being in the real world; he was completely powerless.

"That's the least of your worries!" Evie moved briskly, passing the snake and moving deeper into the forest, towards a clockwork owl that was twitching in some ivy. "Come on, Bren! We need to get the watch so you can get out of that room!"

They began to run then, following a trail of broken animals that had Bren on the verge of tears. They passed hedgehogs and birds, voles and bats, squirrels and deer, beetles and stoats – all torn into mechanical mess.

"So many of them," panted Bren. "But why...why..."

"You noticed what's gone?" Evie slowed a little, her face still tight and determined.

"What do you mean?"

"Look closer."

Bren slowed down too, squinting at the next couple of creatures they passed. And then he saw it. Parts were missing. Plating and rivets. Wheels and gears. Springs and fabric.

"Some of the components are gone," said Bren. He squatted by half a firefly blinking on and off on the moss, probed it with his fingers. "Even the tiniest cogs – they're not here. But why?"

"Bren, we have to keep moving."

When they both began sprinting again, the light that dappled the ground dimmed and brightened. Nearby ferns coiled and uncoiled, flexing their crystal fronds.

"Featherly," panted Bren. "He's playing with the watch."

"Look!" Evie pointed at a tree further ahead. Pulleys began to turn in their grooves, pulling cables and causing the tree to rise.

Bren didn't need to be told. He overtook Evie and leaped onto the lowest branch while the tree turned anticlockwise. He glanced up and – when he glimpsed a dark circle opening in the sky – his heart missed a beat. But the second he made for the next branch, the hole was gone.

The tree reversed its rotation and sank downwards, along with the hope in Bren's breast. Swearing beneath his breath, he dropped to the ground. Everything became silent and still.

Evie caught up. "Almost," she sighed. "Come on. We need to hurry."

As they ran, Furthermoor shifted in fits around them. The sun between the leaves flared and dulled, flared and dulled, as if the day couldn't make up its mind. Trees near and far turned randomly in the moss, pirouetting slowly like waning dancers. Birds and squirrels zipped clumsily between branches, pausing to release broken, jarring cries.

"I *hate* this!" Bren checked his coat was fully toggled up, then shoved his numbing hands beneath his armpits. "And why's Featherly making it so cold?" He puffed with his mouth, half expecting his breath to turn to fog.

"He's not making it cold."

"Then why do I feel so—"

"It must be from the real world. You're completely exposed, Bren, just sitting still while your body gets colder and colder. I guess you're getting so cold up there you're feeling it down here."

Bren rubbed his palms against his arms, trying to create some warmth. Something caught his eye – something wrong with the root of a nearby tree. He ran to the root before stooping in ivy. "No. No…way." He couldn't stop shaking his head. "He can't be doing this."

"Doing what?" Evie crouched beside him. "Oh my god. Is that what I think it is?"

Bren reached out cautiously, almost frightened to touch the root that was no longer wood. "Is this…concrete?" He shuddered when he made contact. The concrete was coarse and cold to the touch, completely alien to Furthermoor.

"I…I can't believe it," breathed Bren. "It must be Featherly."

Evie's eyes were raised, searching the woods. "That's not all. Over there."

She raised her arm, and Bren saw a tree with a wide, unusual knot in its trunk. He got up and approached the tree – not running now, but stepping nervously through the moss, as if afraid Furthermoor's ground would give way beneath his feet. And as he drew closer, his trembling hand went to his mouth.

Bricks.

Red bricks and grey mortar, like a section of wall framed within the tree's gnarly bark.

Bren turned to Evie. He could feel the colour draining from his face. "This is wrong. This stuff – it can't be… It doesn't belong here. Why's Featherly doing this?"

"I don't know." Evie stepped over roots to get to him. "But it doesn't matter."

"Of course it matters!" Bren's lips clenched. A flush of anger sent the colour back to his cheeks. His eyes flitted from the bricked-up knot to the concrete root. "I made Furthermoor for you, Evie. All this is for *you*. And Featherly's ruining it! He keeps ruining everything!"

Evie held his elbow. "It's nothing you can't fix, Bren, when you have the watch. But the *first* thing we need to do is get you out of that room. If we don't, you're going to freeze to death, okay? So come on. Let's keep going."

She tugged Bren's hand, her fingers hot against his skin. With goosebumps racing up his arms, Bren pushed his hands into his pockets and darted after his sister.

CHAPTER SEVENTEEN
THE FEATHERED THRONE

As Bren and Evie burst into a glade, they reached the trail's destination.

The tunnel tree.

Bren kneeled to catch his breath, eyeing an unfamiliar bluish glow in the opening between the tunnel tree's roots.

"He must be in there."

Evie frowned at the sight. "But how?" she said. "It's just a little burrow. It doesn't go anywhere."

Gripping a root to steady himself, Bren peered into the opening. "It does now. Featherly's turned it into a tunnel."

After stooping through that dark mouth, Bren led the way, crawling down a shallow slope. The wool-moss that usually lined the burrow was gone, replaced by a smooth, glowing layer of sapphire.

Bren peered over his shoulder at Evie, who was following close behind. "Our tunnel tree…" she said. Her voice was quiet and hoarse, and her freckles looked dark on her blue-lit skin. Bren could see her sorrow.

"I know," he said, as heartbroken as his sister. This tree was where they'd hung out in the Peaks, when Evie was still alive. It's where Evie first imagined a mechanical forest, where the seed for Furthermoor was planted.

"Don't worry," said Bren, seething in the bluish light. "We'll fix it."

The tunnel gradually widened around them, with its sapphire melting away to reveal something dark beneath: coarse slabs of a silver-black mineral that could have been metal or rock. Bren and Evie aimed for the purplish glow ahead.

They soon entered a vast underground cavern. It was lined with the same metallic rock, though its depths were lit by geometries of purple gemstone, which burst from the walls like explosions frozen in time.

Bren crouched in shadows. He heard Evie whisper beside him. "You still think Featherly's in here?"

She'd uttered the words so quietly, but they bounced from surface to surface, swelling with every echo, until her whispers filled the cavern.

A coarse reply echoed back: "Indeed I am."

An area of purple dimmed to red at the cavern's edge. Featherly chittered.

"Come along, fleshlings."

Bren glanced at his sister. Her glasses glimmered when she nodded, and they were soon crossing the glass of an underground lagoon.

They reached a cove in the bedrock, small and lit by ruby-studded stalactites. Bren saw Featherly's outline by the cove's rocky wall, black and bristling in crimson light. He was crouching with his elbows between his knees, perched on a dark, prickly mass.

Bren's eyes adjusted to the gloom, and he realized the mass was something like a chair or nest – a shabby, sprawling throne made of moss and gears, chains and feathers. Shards of glass pierced its stuffing like giant blades, and Bren's stomach turned when he saw animal pelts woven into the clutter.

Swallowing his revulsion, he clenched his fists and stepped towards Featherly. "I want my watch back."

Featherly's hood jerked to and fro, twitching between brother and sister. "This thing?" He jiggled the watch in his bony hand, then flipped it up so it flashed before landing in his other palm.

Bren stepped forward again, his hands still balled into fists. "No games. Just give it to me."

"Of course, young master."

And with that, Featherly tossed the watch from his throne, straight into Bren's hands.

Bren held it close, cherishing its familiar shape against

his chest. But he was confused. He'd been expecting some sort of struggle – at least some resistance.

Evie must have felt the same. She moved to Bren's side, squinting at Featherly's hood. "You're giving it back, just like that?"

Featherly ruffled his featherbare wings. "Why ever not, sister fleshling? I only wanted a peek. Such an intriguing little trinket."

Evie was deep in thought; Bren could tell. She pouted slightly while her eyes searched Featherly's cove. "What are you doing down here? What's all this stuff?"

Bren followed her gaze and saw shapes in the shadows: spindly constructions of metal and wire, skeletal and lifeless in the cove's red light. Some looked almost humanoid, while others seemed more animal. Some looked trapped between the two, their metal forms tortured and warped.

"Is this what you've been doing with the parts you've taken from animals?" asked Evie. "Using them to make these...*things*?"

Featherly shifted on the mess that was almost a throne. His wings opened a little and fluttered; black feathers fell in the darkness. "A way to pass time," he rasped. "It seems I have a talent for sssculpture."

Bren turned from the shadowy forms to Featherly. "No. You haven't."

"Don't look so disgusted," hissed Featherly. "This is *your* imagination, young master, not mine."

Bren's free hand clenched in anger, until he shivered from the cold that was sinking into his bones. He clutched Evie's hand. "Let's go. I can get back to the room now."

When she nodded, Bren flashed a scowl at Featherly. "Just stop hurting my animals. And leave Furthermoor alone. I won't ask nicely again."

Featherly cocked his beaked hood at Bren. A dry choking sound echoed across stone; Featherly was laughing.

Bren cocked his head too. "What's so funny?"

Featherly wheezed. "The young lord cuts such a brave figure in his imagination. But he's not so bold when things are real."

Determined to leave, Bren turned away.

"The young master has no such boldness," Featherly went on, "with the one called Sendak…"

Bren snapped his head back to Featherly. "How do you know about that?"

A grey finger extended, pointing at the clock in Bren's hand. "Watching with the watch. It's *all* there, little fleshling. Moments and images from the real world, shimmering for me to peruse as I please."

Evie peered from Featherly to Bren. "Hang on… Is he talking about…Mrs Sendak? Did something happen at school?"

Bren shook his head. "It's nothing. We need to go."

Featherly cackled. "Something and nothing, yes-yes-yes. Something because the young master helped Cary again; nothing because he was too cowardly to help himself."

"Stop it," growled Bren.

"It's a miracle the young lord can stand on his feet. To stand up you need some spine."

"Stop. It."

"It's almost as if the poor skulk *wants* to be pushed around."

"*Just stop it!*"

Bren's shout echoed around the cavern. He leaned towards Featherly's throne and opened the watch.

Featherly cackled. "Going to *lash* out again, little lord? You left a pretty scar before." He tapped his hood and leaned towards Bren in return, seemingly daring him to twist those cogs.

Bren's finger hovered by the watch, trembling with rage while his chest heaved. But he couldn't do it. He didn't *want* to do it. So he snapped the watch shut.

"And there we see it again," spat Featherly. "Spineless. Clawless. A snivelling runt. Enjoy reality when you get back, young master. You deserve *everything* you get there."

Bren's knuckles were white. His entire body clamped up when someone pulled his hand, until he realized it was Evie.

"Ignore him, Bren," she hushed, squeezing his fingers. "He's not worth it." Her tone was soft, but she couldn't hide the quiet fury in her voice. "Let's get you back to that room. We don't know how much time you've got left."

Bren took a long breath before swallowing deeply. With the tightness leaving his jaw, he nodded at his sister. He wanted nothing more than to be away from Featherly.

Evie led the way. Without even a glance back, they left Featherly's cove, crossed the lagoon and entered the tunnel.

As soon as they'd left the blue light and were back in the forest, Bren got straight to work with the watch's cogs. He was puzzled by a moment's lag while he adjusted the mechanism, but with a twisting of pulleys and cables, a nearby tree was soon rising.

And above the tree's tip, an opening to the thinking room.

"Go," said Evie, slapping Bren's back and sending him running.

He clambered up branches, glancing down to break into a smile for Evie. She was clapping happily, hopping up and down, but Bren's smile slipped when he saw something dark in the hillock of wool-moss: Featherly's hood, jutting from the tunnel to watch Bren climb.

Bren looked away. He raised his eyes and kept going, and was soon heaving himself through a hole in the sky.

Chapter Eighteen
Return

Tock.

Tick.

Tock.

Tick.

Bren stirred on something damp and springy, opening his eyes to cold darkness.

For a moment he was confused. He fumbled his watch into his pocket, before his hands – one gloved and numb, the other bare and sore – patted his torso and legs.

They moved to the mattress beneath him. He was back in the thinking room, but he could barely see. It must have been night-time.

He had to get out.

Remembering Evie's idea, Bren dragged himself to his backpack, fumbling about blindly. When he found his lunch box he got to his feet and hopped on the spot a few times, trying to shake the cold from his bones. Then he hobbled in the direction of the window, groping in darkness. His fingers met the frosty wall, so he shuffled sideways until he felt cold glass.

Bren pulled back his arm and slammed the lunch box into the window. There was a chiming thud and crack. Bren's hopes rose, before he skimmed the smooth glass – still intact – with his fingers, and then his lunch box. The lunch box's corner had crumpled. It was never going to smash through the window.

He threw it to the floor. Time for plan B.

Bren felt his way to the door. He tried the handle again, just in case, but it was as stuck as before. He got to his knees, probing until he felt a keyhole, then put his mouth to the hole and breathed. After several breaths he jerked the handle, but still the door wouldn't budge.

Bren breathed again, more rapidly now as panic swelled in his lungs. When he rattled the handle he thought he heard something – just the faintest click from the lock. He let out a shuddering yelp of joy. Something had changed with the heat from his mouth.

Bren breathed into the keyhole again, a little hysterical now, laughing-almost-weeping at the thought of making it out. Then he rattled the handle and – after hearing a dull clunk – managed to tug the door open.

He staggered onto the landing. His heart raced with

giddiness. Tears of gratitude were welling in his eyes.

Feeling about with his hands, Bren found his way downstairs and through the hallway and kitchen. He was soon stumbling through the garden and alleyway, but still had to make his way gingerly up Bradbury Avenue, for none of the street lights were on.

When he reached the Dale, he saw that all the houses were dark; not a single light in any window. It must have been really late; the early hours of morning. Mum and Dad – they'd be so worried.

Picking up his pace, Bren turned onto Herbert Road and lurched through the snow. When he reached number forty-seven he saw that the living room light was on. With his teeth chattering, he knocked at the door.

It flew open the instant he touched it. Silhouettes moved in the doorway. Mum and Dad.

"Bren!" Mum's red hair caught the light. "Where on *earth* have you been? Are you okay?"

Before Bren could answer he was huddled inside. Dad shut the door while Mum held Bren close. "My god, you're so cold! What on earth happened? Where have you been?"

"Got...trapped."

"Trapped?"

Bren's thoughts were as sluggish as his limbs, but quickened when he remembered Shaun's warning about grassing. He tensed in Mum's arms, trying to think something up. "At school."

Dad was holding him as well now, in a grip that was as rigid as it was awkward. Bren shivered in his arms, too numb to feel even a hint of his parents' warmth.

"You were trapped at school?"

Bren winced when Mum wiped his damp hair aside. Her fingers felt rough and hard against his forehead. It must have been the cold. His nerves felt dull and raw all at once.

"Was...in the music room," he replied. "Playing guitar with headphones on. Didn't hear the caretaker locking up."

"Why didn't you phone us?"

"My phone died."

"You need to keep it charged, Bren. You never know when you'll need it." Mum pulled the wet shoes and socks from Bren's feet. "You're back now. That's what counts." She guided him upstairs to the landing.

"Shall I run a hot bath?" called Dad from below.

"That'll do more harm than good when he's this cold. He needs warming gently." Mum gave Bren's hand a squeeze so hard he almost gasped in pain. "So you found a way out of that room?" she asked.

Bren swayed with a wave of dizziness. His mum was taking off his coat and clothes, helping him into thick plaid pyjamas. "Yeah," he croaked.

The bedroom was dark, so he only saw Mum's outline while she got him into bed and put on some extra blankets. "Well thank goodness you did." The bed creaked when she sat on its edge. "Just try to warm up and rest now. I'll stay here while your dad gets a hot-water bottle going. You'll be..."

Bren closed his eyes and Mum's words faded away. He'd never been so tired. His numb arms were shivering beneath the blankets.

Weariness took over and sent him deep into sleep.

PART FIVE
THURSDAY

Chapter Nineteen

Pale Skies

When Bren woke up he was still cold.

The bedroom was bright with the light from the window. He scrunched himself up beneath his quilt and blankets, trying to rub some warmth into his toes. When that failed, he squinted at the coat and clothes on the floor from last night.

After rummaging through his school trousers, he was soon back in bed with the watch in his hand. It was eleven in the morning.

"Mum?" he called. "Dad?"

Footsteps, first on the stairs and then on the landing. The door opened and Dad popped his head into the room. "Hey, matey."

Bren sat up. "I'm late for school."

Dad shook his head. His greying hair tumbled around his forehead. "You're not going anywhere. Mum called the emergency doctor last night. You need to stay in bed."

"For how long?"

"Until we say so. A few days, at least."

Bren blinked. There was something unusual in Dad's tone, more forceful than he'd heard in a long time. But Bren didn't mind staying put. He was glad to have a few days off school. A few days away from Shaun.

"Try to sleep," said Dad flatly. He was smiling now from the doorway, though his expression jarred unnaturally against his tone. He must have been uncomfortable; giving orders wasn't usually his thing. "The doctor said the more rest the better."

Bren eased his head back onto the pillow. "If you say so."

"Shout if you need anything."

When the door closed, Bren stayed put and let his gaze wander the room, taking in the wardrobe and desk and the posters on the walls. Then, after a deep breath, he took his watch out from beneath the blanket. He had to tell Evie he'd made it out of the thinking room – that he was home with Dad and safe and sound.

He held the watch to his ear, heard the seconds passing by.

Tick.

Tock.

Tick.

Tock.

And yet: nothing.

Bren closed his eyes and let the ticking go on. He held his breath, listening out for the clacking from the wardrobe.

But it didn't come.

Bren frowned. Why wasn't the watch working? Was he too weak? Was his tiredness affecting him?

With the watch still clutched in his palm, he threw the quilt aside and dragged himself out of bed. He felt dizzy when he stood, and wrapped a blanket tightly around himself to fend off the cold. Feeling a little less groggy with each step, he traipsed across the room to the window.

Bren looked out in time to see someone walking on the other side of the road. When he realized who it was he darted out of sight. Then he crept closer again, peering discreetly from the window's edge.

It was Shaun's dad, strutting through the snow in his trainers. He was wearing the same grey joggers from the other day, and his black bomber jacket was wide open, even though it looked freezing out there. Long spikes of ice hung from the guttering, and the slush lining the road had hardened into dirty grey rocks. The heather in number forty-four's flower basket had been reduced to black stumps. Parked cars and wheelie bins glittered with frost.

The sky above the rooftops looked bleached of colour, with no blue to break its foggy white.

Lowering his eyes, Bren watched Shaun's dad again, and sighed with relief when he disappeared from sight further up the road.

But with Shaun's dad gone, Bren noticed how still everything was.

Not just still, but silent too.

Bren opened the window – just a crack – to listen out. He couldn't hear anything. Not a sound.

Was this how quiet the street was when everyone was at school?

But it wasn't only outside that was quiet. There was no noise from the house either. Nothing from his dad downstairs – no babbling TV or music or radio. No sounds of housework or cleaning – something Bren knew his dad spent most weekdays doing.

Frowning, Bren sat on his bed and tried the watch again.

Tick.

Tock.

Tick.

Tock.

Nothing.

Grunting with frustration, Bren slipped the watch into his pyjama pocket. He didn't want to be here, stuck in his bedroom. The house was too quiet, his room too small. He wanted to be with Evie, in the glass meadow or on the sparkling lake.

As frustrated as he was, Bren did his best to focus on that feeling – on the annoyance. He preferred it to the creeping dread that was gnawing his gut; the chilling, nauseating prospect that, somehow, for some reason, he couldn't get back to Furthermoor.

Trying to push his anxiety aside, Bren made for the door. The moment he opened it he heard footsteps on the stairs. His dad eyed him from the landing's edge. "Why are you out of bed?"

Bren shrugged. "Thought I'd come down for a bit. Maybe watch some TV?"

Dad shook his head. "Stay in bed. Doctor's orders. So go on. Get some rest."

"Can I at least have some breakfast?"

"I'll bring something up."

A small huff left Bren's nostrils. He frowned at his dad, trying to figure out why he was being so uptight. Dad just looked straight back at him.

Bren was confused. He thought his dad had given up on eye contact. Ever since they lost Evie his gaze had been sort of jittery, settling on anything except other people.

Bren shrugged. "Sure. Whatever." He reversed back into his room and – feeling more than a little unnerved – eased the door shut and listened out. He heard footsteps heading down the staircase, but they stopped at the bottom, as if his dad were lingering in the hallway.

Bren didn't go to bed. Instead he went back to the window, and was surprised to catch sight of Shaun's dad again, this time swaggering the other way down Herbert Road.

Pulling the blanket tight over his shoulders, Bren watched from the window's edge, feeling more and more certain that something wasn't right – not just with Dad, but with Shaun's dad too.

What was it about Shaun's dad? Was it the way he strode so casually along the ice, unbothered by the cold that still prickled Bren with goosebumps? Or was it the fact that – even though Bren had *never* seen Shaun's dad on Herbert Road before – he'd come this way twice now?

Shaun's dad continued to march through the snow. His stubbly face looked grim beneath his black, backswept hair, his open mouth set in a sneer.

His *mouth*. That was it.

Bren understood what was niggling him. There was no fog coming from Shaun's dad's mouth.

Bren searched his memory, trying to remember the science behind breath fogging up in cold weather. Something to do with condensation. Did fog always come when it was freezing cold? Or did it stop after a while, when your lungs got used to the temperature?

Bren's lips puckered while he tried to remember, but he still wasn't sure. He stroked the watch's outline in his pocket, wishing he could talk to Evie. She always knew this kind of stuff.

After standing there for some time, Bren turned away and searched his desk. He soon returned to the window with an old rubber stress ball. He'd decided to conduct an experiment.

Opening the window, he yanked back his arm and threw the ball as far down the road as he could. After watching it bounce and roll on the ice, he closed the window, opened the door and called out. "Dad?"

There'd been no need to call. Dad had started up the steps the moment the door opened. He frowned at Bren from the top of the staircase. "Why are you out of bed?"

"Sorry. I'll get back in, I promise. But could you do me a teeny-weeny favour first?"

"What favour?"

"Could you go out and fetch my stress ball?"

"Stress ball?"

"It's just down the road. I threw it from the window."

"Why did you do that?"

"I..." Bren bit his lip, thinking fast. "I was trying to hit some icicles."

An unfamiliar twitch tugged Dad's eyebrow. His expression darkened. "That's a stupid thing to do."

Bren felt suddenly colder than before. This wasn't the Dad he knew. He swallowed drily, trying to hide his nerves.

"Sorry. I wasn't thinking. But could you go get the ball back?"

"You don't need it. Go to bed and stay there."

"Pleeeease, Dad. I really like that ball. I've had it a long time. I don't want anyone to take it."

"No one's going to take it."

"I *swear* I'll go straight to bed as soon as it's back. I won't get up again. I promise."

Dad scrutinized him silently, once again meeting his eyes. But then he nodded. "I'll get it. But only if you get into bed and *stay* there. No more messing about."

Bren put his hands together in gratitude. "Sure! Thanks, Dad."

Dad eyed Bren again before heading down the stairs.

The second he was out of sight, Bren darted to the window. He heard the front door opening below, and saw the top of his dad's scruffy, greying head as he stepped onto the pavement.

Dad looked right, scanning the road, then turned his head left. He must have seen the ball; he started walking.

Bren watched, with his mouth falling open. Something was definitely wrong here. Dad had just gone from the house into freezing cold air but – just like Shaun's dad – no fog came from his mouth. As if he wasn't breathing.

This couldn't be right. Bren's stomach tightened; an unwelcome suspicion was brewing in his mind.

Thinking of how dark it had been last night – of how he'd barely been able to see much of Williamsborough – Bren sped to his bedroom door. He opened it and leaned out, scrutinizing the landing, checking for anything out of place. He saw the old carpet and banister. The scuffed walls. The usual two doors: one to the bathroom, the other to Mum and Dad's room.

All seemed normal.

All seemed fine.

Perhaps he was getting confused about foggy breath. Maybe he was still ill from last night. Tired and paranoid.

But as Bren drew back into his room, something caught his eye. A tiny green twinkle, high on the wall by the edge of the staircase. Something shiny had caught the light from Mum and Dad's room.

Bren took a small step onto the landing, squinting while the thing scuttled across the wall.

The breath caught in his throat.

It was a spider. A spider with a jewelled abdomen and spindly brass legs – all eight of which rippled mechanically as it scurried away.

Bren had no doubt. This wasn't home. This was Furthermoor.

CHAPTER TWENTY
TRUSTING EVIE

Sudden sounds: someone speeding up the stairs, quickly but quietly.

Overcome by dizziness, Bren stumbled backwards into his room, shutting the door as he went and staggering to the window. Glancing out, he saw that whoever was heading up the stairs couldn't be his dad. Dad – or the thing that was *pretending* to be Dad – was still some way down the road, stooping to pick up the stress ball.

Those footsteps were crossing the landing, and Bren turned in time to see his sister burst through the door. He tipped sideways and caught the windowsill in his grip, just as his legs threatened to give way beneath him.

"*Evie*," Bren croaked. He felt hot tears rushing to his eyes. Seeing her here, in their old bedroom...

He blinked as hard as he could. "What's... What's happening?"

Evie clutched his free hand, dragging him from the window. "No time. We need to deal with that...that *thing*."

"Thing?" echoed Bren. He swayed where he stood. Thoughts were swirling around his head, and he pushed his palms against his temples, trying to slow them down.

"That thing out there," Evie went on, "is one of Featherly's machines. It's dangerous and it'll be back any minute."

Bren glanced about the room, still struggling to grasp what was happening. "So this...this isn't the real world?"

Evie shook her head. "It's a copy of Williamsborough, Bren. Built by Featherly using the watch."

"But I...*I've* got the watch." Bren fumbled in his pocket and showed it to her.

Evie snatched the watch from his hand. "Have you tried going to Furthermoor with this?"

"Yeah, but—"

"It didn't work. Cos you've been tricked. You never left Furthermoor and this watch is a fake." Evie gave it a shake. "It's a decoy made by Featherly. To trick you while he keeps the real watch for himself." She shoved the watch into the pocket of her summer dress. "Now let's deal with that dad thing, or it'll never let us out of here."

"Deal with it?" Bren rubbed his eyes, trying to force some composure into his face.

"As in...trap it or something."

"But we can't. There's nothing in here for…trapping stuff." He looked around, almost unable to believe this wasn't his real room.

"We'll have to improvise."

The door slammed shut downstairs, hard enough to make the window rattle.

Evie moved quickly. "Get this on. You'll need it outside." She snatched Bren's duffel coat from the floor and threw it at him. With the blanket falling from his shoulders, Bren slipped the coat over his chequered pyjamas.

They heard footsteps then, coming up the stairs.

Evie eyed the wardrobe, which faced Bren's desk from the opposite wall. "Get the dad thing to stand in front of your desk," she whispered, dragging Bren's chair aside. "Make sure it doesn't look backwards or it'll see me."

The footsteps were on the landing now, getting closer and closer. Evie squeezed herself against the side of the wardrobe not visible from the bedroom door. Bren stared at her, mouthing a tense, "*What?*"

"*Trust me,*" she mouthed back.

Before Bren could say more, the door opened. Bren's eyes darted from the wardrobe to the thing that wasn't Dad. It was studying him with an expression so hard and alien it made his skin crawl.

"You look flustered," it said. "Why are you wearing your coat?"

Bren realized there was something off about its eyes. He could see now how dead they were – how marble-like and cold. He saw the stillness in the dad thing's chest. It definitely wasn't breathing.

Bren pulled his coat close and gave a genuine shiver. "It's just warmer."

The dad thing let the stress ball bounce and roll across the floor. When it spoke, its tone was menacing, emotionless. "Get back into bed. Stay there."

Bren remembered what Evie had told him to do. It took all his willpower not to glance towards her on the hidden side of the wardrobe.

"I will, Dad, I promise. But something's keeping me awake."

"What's keeping you awake?"

"Can you come in? It'll be easier to show you."

The dad thing started to cock its head. Its face kept on tipping, to a severe, unnatural angle. The sight triggered a wave of nausea that forced Bren to push a hand against his stomach.

The thing entered the room, its hard eyes narrowing at Bren. "So, what is it?"

Bren moved stiffly to the desk, opened its drawer and beckoned the thing over. Evie was still poised by the wardrobe.

"Here," said Bren. "This is why I can't sleep."

The dad thing peered towards the window, crossed the carpet and stopped in front of the desk. "What?"

"Keep looking. You'll see it."

While the dad thing frowned into the drawer, Bren shot a discreet glance at the wardrobe. He saw it tip forward slightly before tipping back again, and grasped Evie's plan. With his heart racing, he dashed to the wardrobe's free side to help his sister.

As the dad thing turned its head, Bren stretched both arms to grip the wardrobe's rear corner and – heaving with all his strength – helped Evie to send it toppling forward.

The thing finished turning round and – with its mouth flapping open – tried to leap aside. But it didn't make it. The wardrobe came crashing down, forcing the dad thing backwards. There was a loud crunch – a violent crack of wood against metal – and the thing's waist was pinned between the wardrobe and the desk.

The thing that wasn't Dad writhed like a trapped bug, whirring its arms and lashing out at the siblings. A horrific, distorted snarling came from its throat, like cracked sounds from a broken doll's voice box. Evie clambered over the wardrobe's sloped back, causing the snarls to judder and wheeze.

"Come on!" shouted Evie, already at the door.

Bren stood transfixed by the writhing dad thing, until it blinked and stared at him with eyes suddenly pure white.

The sight sent Bren sprinting out of the room. He hurtled down the stairs after Evie.

"Get some shoes on," she hissed.

Bren peered about while jamming boots onto his feet, baffled by how identical this house was to his own. The living room and kitchen, the coat rack and hallway – it was all exactly the same.

Evie barged the front door open. "Let's go."

They hit the pavement and turned left, making for the Dale at the top of the street. Peering backwards as he rushed through the snow, Bren clocked Shaun's dad watching from across the road. His heart missed a beat when he realized this thing couldn't be Shaun's dad.

"Evie," he panted, still looking over his shoulder.

The shaun-dad's head turned slowly to follow them, then blinked its eyes into marble whiteness. With its eerie, blank expression set on Bren, the thing dropped to all fours.

Bren heard a loud clacking – mechanical and coarse – over his frantic breaths and the crunch of his boots. The sound came from the shaun-dad; its shape was changing. Its stocky forearms bent and shortened, with the fingers at their ends hooking into claw-like curves. The clacking went on, louder now as its spine stretched out, rising at the hips and dipping towards the shoulders. The thing's thick, muscly neck lifted while those shoulders lowered, allowing that blank, stony gaze to stay fixed on Bren.

As soon as its hind legs finished cracking into shape, the shaun-dad thing bolted forward, loping with a body still human in form but dog-like in shape. The clacking noise grew louder as it ran, accelerating into a rattling thrum.

Bren caught up with Evie, screaming as he ran. "That thing! Shaun's dad! It's coming!"

With its bomber jacket flailing wildly, the creature loped across the road and up the pavement, gaining on Bren and Evie even as they sprinted. For all the speed and fierceness of its gallop, the thing's face was cold and impassive, as blank as its eyes.

"It's catching up!" cried Bren. They were at the top of Herbert Road now, nearing a car parked on the corner where the road met the Dale.

Evie's bare feet kicked up snow as they closed in on the car. When she looked quickly over her shoulder, Bren did the same. He saw the shaun-dad catching up fast, its shoulder blades rolling while it loped across the ice.

"It's too fast!" shouted Evie.

Bren was a little ahead of her now, glancing in all directions for anything that could help them. He'd almost reached the car on the corner, and as he passed an alley with a wheelie bin in its shade, he called back to his sister. "In that alley!" He gestured frantically with his hand. "Push the bin into the path!"

"*What?*"

"Do it!"

He could tell from Evie's face that she didn't understand, but she skidded and veered into the alley.

With his duffel coat flapping around his pyjamas, Bren slipped to a stop by the car and spun to see the shaun-dad just metres away. Its lifeless eyes were still locked on him while it loped. Bren did his best to stay put; to ignore every instinct that screamed at him to run. He thought of Cary, scaring that crow from his garden, standing tall against Shaun – tried to summon that nerve.

But Bren didn't have it in him. He shifted his feet, on the brink of fleeing, when something green appeared at the alley's edge. It was the wheelie bin. Evie shoved it out onto the pavement, right into the shaun-dad's path.

The thing's face had no expression, but there was panic in its limbs. It clawed the ice and pedalled backwards with its legs, but the slippery path gave no hold. Bren gawped as the shaun-dad smashed full pelt into the bin.

The bin seemed to explode on impact. The lid flew off and its plastic sides crumpled, sending the bin's contents – binbags and cans and chunks of glittering gemstone – flying through the air and scattering on snow.

The shaun-dad kept its fierce momentum, lifting into the air in a near-somersault. Bren was almost too stunned to move, but managed to stagger out of the way when it crashed into the car's side. The air rang with a crunch that knocked the frost from the car.

With his limbs trembling, Bren stepped back from the broken thing that twitched on the pavement. He heard soft footsteps in the snow; Evie was soon by his side.

She took his hand, panting. "Wow. You okay?"

Bren gaped at the twisted machine, which stared back with eyes like orbs of stone. One of its legs kept turning in its socket, clacking in circles Bren wished would stop.

"Not really," he answered.

Evie tapped the thing's twitching hand with her toe. "It's mechanical. Like the dadalike."

"Dadalike?"

"The thing in your room that looks like Dad. Lookalike, dadalike." Evie gestured to the binbags and gemstones on the snow. "Good thinking, by the way – using the bin to stop this thing."

Bren swallowed the bile that rose beneath his tongue. The shaking in his voice had nothing to do with the cold. "Figured we could...use its speed against it."

Evie nodded in approval. "And using yourself as bait... That must've took some guts."

For all of Evie's talk about guts, Bren couldn't bear to keep looking at the thing on the ground. So he turned his head away.

What he saw made his chin drop.

Chapter Twenty-One

Replica

Bren froze at the sight of Williamsborough Dale, stretching out before him. Or at least, a section of it.

He saw houses and shops on both sides of the road: the nail salon and bookies; the newsagent's and chippy; the kebab shop and pub; the bank and bus stops. But all of it was so silent, so still.

And there in the distance, where the Dale usually reached Williamsborough Academy, the road gave way to a stained-glass meadow, dull with frost and shrouded in fog.

Evie let out an appreciative whistle. "Credit where credit's due – Featherly's really got the hang of that watch."

It took some moments for Bren to find his tongue. "I… I don't get it."

"Hm?"

Bren was struggling to gather his thoughts. "How can

I even be here? In Furthermoor? I climbed through that hole – back into the real world."

"I guess you didn't. Not for real."

Bren scratched his head, narrowing his eyes. "Featherly had the real watch all along. I just had the copy. He's in control of Furthermoor now. He must have sent me to this fake Williamsborough, right here in the meadow."

He peered back towards his house, then scrutinized the bus stops and shops. "I mean, just look at all this! It's immense. Featherly tried to trick me. He wanted me to think I'd made it back into the real world. But…why? Why go to all this trouble?"

"This is *your* imagination, Bren. You tell me."

Bren frowned, unable to make sense of it all. He turned to Evie. "What happened here? I mean, after I climbed through that hole?"

Evie puffed up her cheeks before blowing out some air. "Well, when you disappeared, the sky went dark – like, really dark – and Featherly crept out from the tunnel tree, all caws and cackles and showing off the real watch. Then he sent that thing after me." She pointed over her shoulder to the clicking shaun-dad. "Featherly must have built it, along with the dadalike. Those metal things we saw under the tunnel tree, in the shadows in Featherly's cove… Maybe they were his works-in-progress."

The thought sent a queasy turn through Bren's stomach.

"I ran into the forest," continued Evie, "and the running thing came after me. But it doesn't know the woods like I do, and I guess the darkness helped me out. I stuck to the undergrowth. Made it to the lake to hide."

"You hid in the lake?"

"In that bit where the deckchair flips up. I hid in the gap underneath. And then, when daylight returned, I crept back out. And guess what I found."

Bren nodded towards the Dale. "All this?"

"I saw Ballard Tower first. In the distance. Or at least most of it, like it was under construction or something." Evie's eyes went wide. "Can you imagine what it was like, Bren, seeing the estate sticking out from the treetops in Furthermoor?"

Bren's eyes were back on the shops – on the bus stops and frosty slate rooftops. "I guess I can."

Evie went on. "I was heading for the tower, sticking to cover, but when I passed the meadow it wasn't the same. There were terraced houses, like these, in the middle of all the flowers. And I recognized the streets. I saw…"

Evie hesitated. Bren looked across and saw her eyes watering. She lifted her glasses to wipe away a tear.

"I saw home, Bren. I was home."

Bren squeezed his sister's hand. Her expression hardened. "But it wasn't really home. It couldn't be. This is Furthermoor."

Bren was rubbing his chin, thinking back. "The concrete..."

"Concrete?"

"Yeah. The concrete root we saw in Furthermoor, on the way to Featherly's cavern. Do you remember? We saw red bricks too, in a knot in a tree. Featherly must have been practising." He waved his finger in a circle in the air. "Getting ready for all this." Bren grimaced bitterly. "And it looks like he's a natural."

Evie nodded. "When I recognized the streets, the first place I wanted to go was our house. I had to sneak up Herbert Road, hiding behind the bins and cars, cos this thing –" she threw a look at the broken shaun-dad – "was patrolling the streets. When I saw the dadalike leave the house I snuck in. And that's where I found you, about to faint in your pyjamas."

Bren rubbed his forehead, still stunned by it all, until he was struck by a thought that had him grabbing his sister's arm. "Evie, there's another one of these machines – one that looks like Mum! It put me to bed last night!"

Evie stiffened, her eyes flitting across the streets. "That'd make sense."

"So where is it now?" With a shudder, Bren thought back to the previous night – to the lack of any physical warmth from his parents, to his mum's hard, clunky caress.

"Maybe it's gone for now," said Evie, though Bren heard

the worry in her voice. "She'd normally be at work now, right?"

Bren hugged himself while a chill crept up his spine. "I guess. Or maybe it's here somewhere, patrolling like the other one was." He glanced backwards at that still-whirring leg, those stone-white eyes.

Evie took his hand and began to walk. "We need to move, Bren."

Bren stumbled behind her. "Where are we going?"

"Well, where are you right now?"

"I'm...I'm here."

"I mean your real body. If you didn't actually make it out of Furthermoor, where's your real body?"

Bren sucked in a gasp of cold air. "I'm in the thinking room!" He gaped at his sister. "Oh god. Do you think I'm...I might be...dead?"

Evie shook her head. "If you were dead we wouldn't be here. You wouldn't be able to imagine this. But we don't know how much time's passed in the real world. You could have hypothermia by now. You might be close to dying. You're in danger, Bren." She chewed her bottom lip. Bren noticed how the skin around her freckles had paled.

"So we're back to square one," he said. "We still need to get the watch off Featherly, so I can get back to the *real* real world and find a way out of that room." He squinted at the forest in the distance. "Do you know where Featherly is?"

"Not for sure. But I'm guessing he's at the tunnel tree, maybe in that cavern."

Bren's gaze drifted north. He was trying to visualize the tunnel tree's position in this fake Williamsborough. "That'd be...by Ballard Tower?"

"That's where we're heading."

As they picked up their pace, Bren craned and twisted his neck, taking in this replica of the world he so desperately had to get back to. They crossed the road at the top of Bradbury Avenue, and Bren peered at its boarded windows and satellite dishes. A cold flush made him shiver beneath his duffel coat. When he pushed a hand through his hair, his fingers felt raw and icy against his scalp.

Something moved. Across the road. Bren clutched Evie's hand tighter, bracing himself for the mum thing from last night. But his grip loosened when he saw a clockwork fox. Its felt and copper joints shone briefly in the light, before it vanished behind a bin bristling with frost.

He heard Evie whisper. "Some of these streets weren't here earlier. Or they weren't as long. This Williamsborough's still growing."

After crossing a couple more streets, they turned left onto Lewis Road – the street that led to Ballard Tower. As with Williamsborough Dale, Bren saw the road ahead give way to glass meadow, which in turn gave way to emerald forest. And there, breaking through the canopy and dominating the landscape: Ballard Tower.

"It's changed," murmured Evie. It didn't look half-built – not like when she'd first seen it. Ballard Tower had its full height now. One of its glass-and-concrete sides gleamed green with crystal ivy, and the exposed, bridge-like corridors connecting the lift tower to the main block were sheathed in sapphire. And at its top...

Bren's heart stopped at the sight of a huge tree, raised high into the sky by the concrete column.

"Is that our tunnel tree?" he whispered. "On top of the tower?"

"It is," said Evie, in a tone Bren knew well. It was the sound of his sister trying to be strong, unable to hide her pain. To see their tree raised up like that, torn from the ground...

Bren squinted. Something else was wrong. The tree's trunk and branches looked different, somehow. Their silhouettes were chunky and coarse – though from this distance, it was hard to tell why.

A nearby noise broke the silence: sounds of clawing and cawing, coming from an alleyway to the left. While Bren hesitated, Evie released his hand and crept towards the alley. After peering round its corner, she ran in and coarse squawks filled the air.

Bren sprinted to the alley, and saw a mechanized crow –

as big as a dog, with eyes of ruby fire – hopping and flapping in the shadows, trying to peck a squirrel that lay sprawled on the ground. Evie was kicking at the bird with all her might.

Bren stood and gawped, unable to enter the alley. The crow's eyes flashed right at him, and his mind raced with memories of beaks and claws. He couldn't bring himself to get any closer.

Evie had no such fear. She grunted and lashed out with her bare feet, until a hard wallop against the crow's chest sent it flapping from the alley. Bren had to cover his face and duck as it soared past.

With the crow gone, Evie got her breath back and returned to her brother. He opened his mouth, about to say sorry for hanging back, but Evie put her palm up. "It's okay. I get it."

With a rush of fear tightening his mouth, Bren lifted his gaze to search the sky. "Do you think...there are more of them?"

"Could be." Evie took his hand again, looking at him seriously. Bren looked back at her, taking in the copper waves of her hair – her high, freckled cheekbones and feline eyes – and thought again of how much she looked like Mum.

A wave of sadness hit him hard; a near-physical pang he could feel in his chest. He missed his parents so much.

Evie squeezed his hand. A smile tugged the edge of her mouth. "You know, I'm amazed you're scared of crows. I'm amazed you're scared of anything."

"*What?*" Bren almost laughed, though he felt a little hurt. "You're making fun of me."

"I'm deadly serious."

Bren's gaze went to his feet. "Stop it."

"I mean it, Bren." Evie jiggled his hand. "Honest, all the stuff you've been through... You know, with Shaun and now Cary, and the crows and –" her voice cracked – "what happened to me... If it'd been the other way round and I'd lost you..." She cleared her throat. "A lot of people would have fallen to pieces. But not you."

Bren stared at some ice. "You think I wasn't in pieces?"

"You were. But you picked them up. You're so much stronger than you think. So much braver."

Bren snorted an awkward laugh. "Brave," he spat, though he couldn't help thinking back to Cary's garden – to when Cary had called him brave too.

"I'm a wimp," he muttered. "I just...hide from everything."

"You *are* brave. Look at me."

When Bren lifted his eyes, Evie looked so stern. He felt another pang for Mum and realized how much he'd been missing her, even in the real world. She'd thrown herself into work after Evie died, and was always busy, always distracted. And Dad may have been home, but in some ways he wasn't. His thoughts were always elsewhere; he'd become so distant – so uneasy and fragile.

Evie tapped Bren's hand. "Bravery isn't always big and loud, Bren. It can be quiet too. So would you do me a favour?"

"What?"

"Give yourself a break sometimes, yeah?"

Her expression was so severe that Bren couldn't help a nervous laugh. Evie's frown faded and she chuckled too, until her gaze returned to the alley.

"Oh god." Her frown was back. "That squirrel, Bren… Do you see what I see?"

Chapter Twenty-Two
Lateral Thinking

Bren entered the alley to crouch by the squirrel, brushing aside torn flaps of felt. The wire mesh beneath was splayed to reveal cogs, gears and sprockets unlike any Bren had ever seen. Rather than being metallic, they were a dry, chalky off-white.

He touched a pale cog before whipping his hand back in disgust. "The mechanism," he breathed. "It's all made of bone."

Bren twisted to look up at Evie, who was frowning at the squirrel's white, skeletal machinery.

"Featherly," she said. "Maybe he's trying to make meat. Flesh and blood, like he always wanted." She turned to face Ballard Tower. "Let's keep going. You can fix all this when you get that watch back."

The siblings continued down Lewis Road. The further they went, the more the houses looked unfinished. Each building had fewer roof tiles and beams than the last, and when there were no roofs, the upper floors followed suit, exposing crude joists and girders. Bren soon found himself surrounded by icy building materials. He saw half-formed brick walls and empty window frames; mounds of breeze blocks and frosty slate.

As the pair went on, the meadow seemed to creep into the fragments of street. It covered stacked joists with crystal weeds and thistles. Bren spotted the occasional metallic insect – brass beetles and nickel dragonflies – buzzing through the air before settling on bricks.

The road was soon behind them. Evie and Bren marched through the meadow, taking old paths that looked likely to lead to the tower. As they closed in on the forest, Bren tried to take some comfort in its familiarity. Apart from being pale with a dusting of ice, the trees and crystal undergrowth looked reassuringly untouched.

But then Bren heard rustling chimes, coming from some distance behind them. When he turned around, that fleeting moment of comfort left him. Something unseen was crashing through the flowers, whipping their stalks as it drew closer. A mechanical clacking began to fill the air.

Evie turned too, her cry launching mechanical sparrows from the trees: "Run!"

Bren shuffled backwards, unable to tear his eyes from the flowers, which thrashed to and fro as if being flailed by a low, scuttling storm. The chime and splinter of a thousand petals rose in pitch, until the mum thing – with a mechanical scream that made Bren's blood run cold – burst through shattered flora onto the path they'd been using.

Just like the shaun-dad, the mumalike had changed its shape for the chase. It hit the path like a pouncing dog, with its hands – now clawed and stretched out – landing first and its contorted legs following.

With a flick of red hair, the mumalike snapped its face up from the path. Those hard white eyes locked onto Bren and it was moving again, loping swiftly on all fours.

"I said *run*!" shouted Evie. Bren felt her hand yank his own, pulling him towards the woods.

They sprinted between trees and ferns, with the meadow behind them and the mumalike closing in. Even over his gasping breaths, Bren heard its clacking thrum, its four-footed gallop against the wool-moss. With a backward glance he saw that the mumalike was gaining on them. Its raised face remained level and blank on its lengthened neck, while its limbs spun in their sockets to send it pounding through ivy.

Bren shrilled at Evie: "*What do we do?*"

"I don't know!"

Another backward glance. The mumalike was drawing nearer still, its suit stretched and torn by its distended spine.

"It's too fast!" cried Bren. "We can't outrun it!"

Evie looked left and right before checking over her shoulder. "And we can't hide! It's too close!"

Bren's lungs were aching. He gasped for air. "It's over!"

"Never!" Evie grimaced and shook her head. "Lateral thinking!"

"Lateral what?" shrieked Bren. That clacking was getting louder. Bren heard the pelt of those clawed, lengthened hands, closer and closer.

"Think from a..." Evie gulped a lungful of air. "A different angle! Only way to escape...getting caught!"

"*What?*"

"I'll let it get me! It can't hold us both! You can make it to the tower!"

"Evie!"

She'd already skidded to a stop and turned around. Bren stopped and twisted too, watching in terror as the mumalike closed in. It didn't react in any way to its prey stopping; it just kept bounding on with fearsome speed.

When Evie jogged towards it, Bren started to follow, until she pushed out a palm and scowled over her shoulder. "No, Bren! Go to the tower! I'm not getting myself caught just so you can mess this up!"

Bren hesitated, still staggering forward behind his sister. "But Evie..."

She was running now, picking up speed and on course for direct collision with the mumalike.

Bren squinted through welling eyelids at the thing that wasn't Mum. He could see specks of white stuffing jutting from its face, where it had been nicked by sharp foliage.

He slowed to a stop. "Evie! What if it *hurts* you?"

Evie glanced backwards, glaring fiercely. "Go get our watch! Mum and Dad have already lost me. I'm not going to let them lose you too!"

As she slammed into the charging mumalike, Bren inched backwards, trying his best to do as Evie had said. His legs seemed to resist, though; each step forced fresh tears into his eyes. Gritting his teeth, Bren forced himself to turn away, then sprinted again.

Glancing over his shoulder, he saw the mumalike – with Evie gripped in one arm – struggling to pursue him. It tried to claw its way forward with its three free limbs, but Evie was pulling its torso and kicking its legs. It wasn't going anywhere.

Bren was free, but he was on his own. Tears were still welling in his eyes, but he wiped them away and kept running, more determined than ever to get his watch.

Evie was right: there was no way his parents could lose him too. And there was no way he could lose them.

They'd all lost too much already.

Chapter Twenty-Three
The Crystal Tower

Bren dashed through a blur of tree trunks, past cogs embedded in moss and ice. He watched his booted feet as he ran, hopping over grooves and dodging crystal ferns.

And then, not far ahead: a slab of grey filling a wide clearing.

The base of Ballard Tower.

When he saw movement in the clearing, Bren stopped and caught his breath. Keeping low behind undergrowth, he crept forward and could soon see the tower's entrance – a glass doorway, framed in concrete at the foot of the lift tower.

But the clearing wasn't deserted.

Bren counted at least a dozen crows – each of them even bigger than the one he'd seen in the alley – perched on the concrete lip above the doorway, or hopping along the clearing's wool-moss. They bristled their sharp black feathers, and Bren sensed from their twitching heads –

from the way they peered about with those glinting, ruby eyes – that these crows were lookouts. Sentries. Guards. Featherly must have made them to protect the tower.

Bren's mouth went dry. He squeezed his eyes shut, trying to quiet his laboured breathing. But when he closed his eyes he saw the crows that had attacked him on Lewis Road – felt the thrash of their wings, the cut of their claws.

The crows in the clearing chattered and rasped. Bren opened his eyes and looked up, taking in what he could of the lift tower's height. He couldn't see its summit from the canopy's edge; only the thin, slitted windows that peppered the tower's front, obscured here and there by rashes of ivy.

He clocked something dark reflected in an upper window, rising and flapping towards the tower's top. It was Featherly, with a silhouetted figure grasped in each hand – one as motionless as a doll, the other writhing in his grip.

Evie.

Bren had to get to Featherly. He had to help his sister, and he had to get that watch.

Squinting ahead, he could just make out the lobby through the tower's doorway. But he had no idea how to get there. The thought of going anywhere near those crows made his stomach churn. And even if it didn't, he wouldn't stand a chance of getting past them. There were too many. They were too fast. They'd tear him to shreds.

Bren pushed his palms against his forehead, wishing

Evie was with him. She'd know what to do. Improvise. Lateral thinking. Something like that.

There had to be a way around this; Bren was sure of it. Cary had called him smart. He'd outwitted Shaun, Alex and Isaiah on Bradbury Avenue – sent them running into alleys while he took Cary to safety.

Bren grimaced, deep in thought.

Improvise…

The answer came to him. It was so obvious. That doorway wouldn't be the only way into the tower.

Bren inched his way along the canopy's edge, circling the clearing as carefully as he could. He skirted the block's side until he saw his way in. A window on the ground floor, at the lift block's rear.

After checking for crows, Bren left the woods and jogged across the clearing. With the canopy now behind him, he could crane his neck to see the tower's full, dizzying scale. It soared upwards into pale sky. Corridors beyond counting bridged the lift tower and the residential block, like gantries connecting a rocket to its launch tower. Most of them were encased in blue crystal, scattering rainbows against the grubby concrete.

A caw from the tower's front turned Bren's jog into a sprint. With goosebumps prickling his skin, he pulled the window open and climbed through, before dropping onto a cold linoleum floor.

He was in the lift tower's lobby. Getting up quickly, Bren eased the window shut and pressed himself against the wall. He slid along with his eyes fixed on the entrance, in case any crows turned their gazes from the clearing to the lobby. When he pressed the button for the first lift, Bren was surprised to see the metal doors open. But rather than revealing a lift, they opened onto a smooth face of rock. The second lift was the same.

Shuffling on, Bren reached a red door. It was unlocked, and when Bren pushed through he saw the bottom of the tower's stairwell.

He'd never used Ballard Tower's stairwell in the real world, but knew for a fact that it wasn't like this. The stairs themselves looked normal: linoleum steps with a metal handrail. But when Bren tiptoed to the stairway's centre and peered upwards, he saw glass ivy clinging to the steps' undersides, pierced here and there by shards of gemstone.

Bren listened out. All he could hear was his rapid breathing. After testing the first step cautiously with his boot, he took the next step and began his ascent.

His legs had been aching even before he'd started to climb. He changed direction with each flight of steps, facing one wall then the next while moving doggedly upwards. Whenever he hit a landing with a corridor, he peered through and saw the passages of the residential block. They looked so real – so humdrum and drab – until

Bren spotted glass weeds creeping from beneath apartment doors. Clockwork dragonflies flitted from tiles and strip lights.

Bren's ascent became sluggish with pain; he'd lost count of the corridors he'd passed. His thighs felt sorer with every step, so he paused on a landing to rest and get his breath back. While rubbing his aching calves, he shuffled to a window and peered out. He was high enough to see Furthermoor stretching away beneath him. The distant meadow was filled with roads and terraces, and to the west he saw the sapphire lake.

The forest was so far below him now. Bren prayed that meant he was close to the tower's top. But when he left the window to squint up the stairwell, the stairs and ivy went on and on. He still had so far to go.

Putting his foot to the next step, Bren kept going.

His feet soon felt blistered in his boots, and his thighs and calves were stiff. Moving slower now but still rising, Bren pulled his coat tight round his pyjamas. He should have been hot from the effort, soaked with sweat. But the further he rose, the colder he became. What was happening to him in the thinking room? How much time did he have left?

A few flights more and Bren could barely walk. He fell forward with a groan, and was soon mounting steps on his hands and knees. When he couldn't go on, he heaved himself onto a landing and rolled onto his back. He lay there panting and shivering – so cold now that it stung his face, hands and toes – and stared tiredly at ivy above.

When Bren tried to get up, he couldn't move. He could almost feel his heart sinking, like a heavy stone pressing against his spleen, weighing him down.

He sensed a speck of warmth on his face: a tear. Bren wiped it away, and saw with horror that his hand was glazed in frost, as if crystallizing in the tower's icy air. He lifted his other hand and whimpered when he saw it was the same.

Again, he tried to get up. But his strength had left him.

Bren knew in this moment that he'd failed. He'd gone as high as he could go. He wasn't getting his watch back and he wouldn't reach Evie. Instead he was going to freeze to death, here and in the real world – stuck on a landing and locked in a room.

Featherly had been right all along. Bren was weak. A living doormat.

Spineless and cowardly.

A skulk.

Which meant Evie had sacrificed herself for nothing. She'd given herself to that hideous mumalike and to Featherly, only to have her brother let her down.

And she'd had so much faith in him.

Evie…

Bren's finger twitched.

He thought again of his sister and it twitched once more. A speck of frost loosened from his hand, before drifting like a snowflake to the floor.

No.

He wouldn't give up.

Still thinking of Evie, Bren tensed his fingers as hard as he could. He felt some warmth and strength returning.

The ice cracked as he balled his hands into his fists, and the thought of his parents – of his *real* parents, who'd be so helpless and worried, who'd already lost their daughter – pushed Bren back to his feet.

Mum and Dad.

Bren was on the next flight of stairs, rising again. He was closer to the tower's peak than he'd realized.

After three more flights there were no stairs left; only the final corridor, leading to the main block's top floor. When Bren entered the corridor he heard a hellish squawking; something flapped against the sapphire crusting the windows. Ducking and wincing, Bren scarpered through the space and into the residential block.

His legs had never hurt so much; he felt as if his very bones were bruised. But he pushed himself on, searching left and right, up and down, for a way to the tower's roof.

While the doors to the flats were all green, the one at the passage's end was a dirty white. Bren barged through into in a space filled with boilers and pipes. He saw a steel ladder at the room's far end and was climbing it in an instant. When he pushed the metal trapdoor at its top, it opened with a clang to a gust of cold air.

Slowly, gradually, Bren lifted his head through the opening.

Chapter Twenty-Four

The Falling Hood

Bren's eyes were level with the tower's flat roof. He saw its surface streaked by branching shadows. He saw huge birds covering every vent and pipe – mechanical crows beyond counting, watching him with their hard red eyes.

Bren's breath caught in his gullet. But he didn't duck or flee, for the sight of the tunnel tree caused gall to overwhelm his fear. The tree – Bren and *Evie's* tree – had not only been ripped from its glade and perched on this tower, but was also slathered in a coat of concrete.

Bren gaped in shock and disgust. The tree's trunk was bound in dirty stone, with its craggy roots sprawling to grip the roof's edge. The concrete crusting its branches had hardened mid-drip, so that it hung above Bren in ugly grey stalactites.

Their tunnel tree – the very seed of Furthermoor, once

so bold, beautiful and green – now looked grotesque, suffocated, disfigured.

And there was Featherly, squatting on his throne not far from the tree's trunk. The throne was the same as before: a hideous, nest-like lump of pelt and feather, chain and moss. Crystal spikes protruded from the mess, with the cold light twinkling on their tips.

A dry, chittering rasp. "Little fleshling…once lord of this land."

Featherly looked changed somehow. His face was still hidden in his beaked hood, and he wore the same skinny jeans and hoodie, but something was different.

Bren didn't get the chance to figure it out, for his eyes were drawn to Evie. She was struggling to the left of Featherly's throne, pulling and heaving, trying to tear herself from the mumalike behind her. It was useless, though. The mumalike – now on its feet and human in shape – stood with its hands locked tight on Evie's arms. The machine was completely motionless – more manacle than mechanical – with its pale marble eyes staring at nothing.

"Bren!"

Evie's cry sent Bren further up the ladder, until the squawk of a crow sent him back down a rung.

"No-no-no," chuckled Featherly, fidgeting on his throne. "Best not duck your head, young master. You want this t-trinket, do you not?"

Featherly raised a crooked arm. Bren saw Evie's watch – the *real* watch – held in Featherly's grey, bony hand.

"Your sssibling too, yes-yes-yes?" Featherly went on. "You'll never get watch and kin by keeping your head down – much as that's your favoured way." A wheezing chuckle.

Evie called again to Bren. "*Don't be—*"

"Silence!" Featherly snapped his fingers, and a crow took to the air before landing at Evie's feet. "Speak again, sister fleshling," hissed Featherly, "and I'll have this bird feast on your tongue."

Bren grimaced. With his eyes flitting between Featherly, Evie and the nearest crow, he left the hatch and stepped onto the roof.

His grimace weakened when the crow hopped towards him. Bren stepped sideways, trying to get some distance, but it hopped forward again, then kept hopping, forcing Bren backwards along the roof, until he was gripping the rail at the summit's edge.

Bren glanced down and swayed on his feet. He'd never been so high – not in real life and not here. The lake and meadow were tiny now. And the jewelled forest went on and on, unfurling to a horizon wider than Bren had ever seen.

With his stomach lurching, Bren released the rail and staggered away from the edge, all the while being careful to step around the crow still watching him. To his relief it stayed put.

When his stomach settled, he took a deep breath and called out to Featherly. "Why?"

Featherly cocked his hood. "Why what, little lord?"

Bren aimed a finger towards the streets in the meadow below. "Why are you doing this?"

Featherly tossed the watch up, catching it in his hand. "Admirable work – is it not?"

"You didn't answer my question."

Featherly held the watch close to his chest. "I'm taking away something you don't deserve."

"And what's that?"

"Sanctuary, little master. Refuge and asylum. A haven of safety and bliss." Featherly gripped the watch tighter. "In a word: *Furthermoor*."

Bren's eyes narrowed. "You think I don't deserve Furthermoor?"

Featherly's answer was a rasping snarl. "Of course you don't! In real life you forever skulk and scuttle. And when you're not skulking and scuttling, you're rolling over for every little tyrant. That's what people like you do, yes-yes-yes. You bow down and bare your soft, stunted backbone for all to see. It's pathetic. So why should you deserve Furthermoor? It's plain hypocrisy."

He gestured to the horizon. "How hollow and wretched it is, young master of none, to *imagine* yourself into power; to puff yourself up in your little crystal forest. It's ssssickening."

Bren was still confused. "But you could have just got rid of Furthermoor. You could have kept me out or...or done anything! Why'd you build a fake Williamsborough?"

"All the better to trap you with."

Bren pointed frantically at the watch in Featherly's hand. "You've got the watch! You can trap me in a million ways!"

Featherly tutted beneath his hood. "For someone who thought up Furthermoor, you sorely lack imagination." His head twitched to one side. "The best prisons, young lord of none, are the ones in which you think you're free. How do you escape a trap you don't realize you're in?"

He fidgeted and cackled then, rubbing his palms between his knees. "It's been verrry satisfying. So much so that I ceased trying to make meat. There are finer things to relish. For I wasn't building *quite* the Williamsborough you know, young fleshling; more the Williamsborough you deserve. I planned some touches of my own. Colder parents. Angrier bullies. Hardship and loneliness...and oh so many crows. A useless watch and no chiming forest to flee to.

"I was going to imprison you, little master, in a Williamsborough even crueller than the one you know."

Featherly began to chuckle then, until the chortling from his hood became a coarse, braying cackle.

Bren was speechless. That laugh had turned his spine into a rod of ice.

"Don't look so forlorn," rasped Featherly. "It's exactly what you've earned. Eternal submission: the only fate fit for a—"

"Stop it, Featherly!" It was Evie. She struggled uselessly against the mumalike, her eyes darting to the crow by her feet. "Give Bren the watch! He doesn't deserve *any* of this!"

The sharp point of Featherly's hood jerked towards her. "But oh, sister fleshling, he does. I know he does. *He* knows he does too."

Though Bren was shaking with cold and horror, the sight of Evie struggling sent a flush of anger through his veins. He stepped towards the throne. "You're wrong, Featherly. You don't know anything about how I feel."

Featherly pulled in a long, wheezing breath. "Oh yes-yes-yes, little lord, I know you. I know you like no one else."

He shivered and cackled then, shifting to get up. As he unfolded his legs to stand on the throne, Bren saw what was different about him. Featherly was taller now, but also scrawnier – as if stretched out on a rack, rather than grown.

Featherly rolled his bony shoulders, chittering with pleasure as he fanned his huge wings. They'd lost their shabbiness and were as broad and black as night. He wafted them gently, sending a foul gust – ripe and thick with scents of decay – coursing over Bren.

"Oh yesssss," hissed Featherly. "I know you better than you know yourself."

And then, after raising a hand to his head, Featherly pulled down his hood.

Bren could only stare in disbelief.

He was looking at himself.

Chapter Twenty-Five

Mirrored

Himself, though not quite.

Featherly had Bren's features, but his face was thinner, gaunter. His eyes were like orbs of black ink; his skin ash-grey; his hair not wavy red but lank and crow-dark. And on his right cheek, a grey scar left by the cable Bren had snapped in anger.

Featherly's lip curled into a skewed smile. Bren kept staring, stunned and silent, trying to process what he was seeing.

"Bren? Featherly's…*you*?" Evie shouted over a gust of chill wind. She'd stopped struggling, and blinked forcefully as if she couldn't believe what she was seeing. "He can't be! He can't be you!" Tears began to well in her eyes. "Is that really how you feel, Bren? That you *deserve* all this?"

"He deserves everything that comes to him," hissed Featherly. "Because he's scared. Because he's a coward." He counted on his bony fingers as he spoke. "Because he never fights back. Because he never stands up for himself. Because he fears *everything* – even asking for help."

Evie's horrified gaze flitted from Featherly to Bren. She shook her head desperately, almost pleading with her brother. "You don't believe that, do you, Bren? Tell me you don't."

Bren opened his mouth but he couldn't reply. Shame filled his throat, blocking the words. There was no denying it. Featherly was Bren – the deepest, darkest part of him – and he spoke a truth Bren could no longer hide from himself.

Evie clamped her eyes shut. Bren saw the tears streaking her cheeks. "Don't do this to yourself!" she wailed, her voice growing hoarse. "Stop treating yourself like this!"

Without even glancing at her, Featherly flipped open the watch and adjusted some cogs.

"I told you!" cried Evie. "Stop being so hard on—" She was silenced by a vile clacking; a third arm had unwound from behind the mumalike, smothering Evie's mouth with a flat, fingerless hand.

Featherly finished for her. "Hard on himself? I think you'll find he should." He rolled his dark eyes at Bren. "Our know-it-all sister – the spanner in my works. Even in death, she's a nuisance."

He peered sidelong at Evie while she struggled against

all three of the mumalike's arms. When his gaze returned to Bren, an unhinged leer warped his face.

"So, young master of nothing, it seems there's no tricking and trapping you in my Williamsborough. Not now. So we'll be rid of you some ssssimpler way."

With a nod of Featherly's head, several crows began to circle Bren. He backed away as the birds drew close, flapping their pitch-black wings, screeching through those blade-like beaks. Bren was being pushed to the roof's brink. Featherly rasped again.

"We share faces but not wings, young lord. My crows will come close and you'll fly one way, all the way to the ground. Do bones break in Furthermoor?" Featherly jiggled the watch. "I'll see to it that they do."

The crows kept drawing in, cawing and clacking their giant beaks. Bren had nowhere to go – nowhere but over the tower's edge. His breaths became jagged, until he heard Evie call again. "Bren!"

He looked over, saw her spitting out cogs. She'd gnawed through the mumalike's hand. Her horror had given way to a steeliness Bren knew well.

"Fight this part of yourself!" she shouted. She wasn't pleading any more; it was an order. "Prove Featherly wrong! I know how brave you really are!"

Bren called back, his voice breaking with shame. "But I'm not, Evie!"

Her red hair flailed in the wind. "Look how far you've come!" She nodded towards the Williamsborough below. "Look at everything you've survived!" She smiled then, flushed with confidence, and Bren saw her faith in him, fiery in those bright, hazel eyes. "You just—"

More clacking and she was cut off again. Featherly shook his head, stepping from the throne with his black, spindly legs.

"Ignore her," he rasped. "She knows more of the grave than of her brother. But *I* –" Featherly drew out the word, grinning with teeth as sharp as the stalactites above – "I *know* you, Bren. Yes-yes-yes, I know how scared you are. We *both* know."

"But..." With a glance at the drop beyond the railing, Bren turned even paler. "But, Featherly! Falling from here will kill me!"

"Yesssss."

"It'll kill...*us*!"

A raised black eyebrow. "Us?"

"If I die here, I die in the thinking room! I'll freeze to death in the cold, and that means no imagination and no you."

Featherly faltered, tucking his wings behind his back. He twitched his head towards the watch, frowning in thought.

"Don't you get it?" shouted Bren. "You need me,

Featherly; you can't live without me! Killing me will kill you!" He stared at Featherly, willing him to come to his senses.

When Featherly lifted his face, Bren saw conflict tugging his eyes and lips. But he ruffled his feathers and gritted his teeth. His broad wings fanned open. "Then so be it."

Bren sensed the sting in his fingers changing, shifting, warming. The cold that had chilled him became a numb throb, as if the blood were running faster in his veins – hotter, quicker, wilder. He looked towards Evie and the mumalike, seething at the thought of how Featherly could do this to his mum, to the memory of Evie.

When he looked again at Featherly – at this grotesque, winged reflection – Bren was overcome by a wave of loathing. He hated Featherly as much as he hated this cruel, pitiless, unforgiving part of himself; this dark truth now bare and exposed, in all its malice and disgust.

Bren's teeth clenched, mirroring Featherly's own. With his chest heaving, he shook his head and stepped towards his feathered twin. "No, Featherly. I *will* leave the thinking room. So give me that watch. I'm getting out of here and I'm going to live."

Featherly sneered. "Hollow words, young faintheart. You don't have it in you."

"I do. You've gone too far. I've had enough."

Featherly chittered and chuckled. His dark wings

fanned out further, beating and swelling while he adjusted the watch. Bren was pushed into the rail by the gust from Featherly's plumes, but he leaned headlong into that sour wind, inching forward again – until the wind stopped and the crows closed in.

Bren hesitated. He felt the chill return to his bones, colder with every flash of those jewelled red eyes. But as the huge birds drew closer, Bren thought once more of Cary – of how he'd scared that crow from his garden. Bren closed his eyes, trying to remember Cary's words.

Bullies are like animals. And animals can smell your fear. So hide it. Puff up your chest, make some noise. Make your bark worse than your bite.

Fake it till you make it.

Bren pulled back his shoulders, forcing himself to meet the gaze of the closest crow. "No," he said, quietly but as firmly as he could. He took a step forward, speaking louder, keeping his eyes locked on the crow's. "*No.*"

To his surprise, the crow hopped backwards, bristling its feathers.

Bren narrowed his eyes at the other birds. "No," he repeated, raising his voice. His heart lifted – just a little – when the crows gibbered and hopped backwards too.

One of the birds – a particularly large one close to Featherly – was less intimidated. Its red eyes and razor beak flashed, catching the light as it launched itself at Bren.

But Bren didn't run. Something was building in his breast – something volatile, feral and fierce. "I said *no*!" he barked, and as the rage rose from his lungs, he realized he wasn't faking it.

The crow swerved with a shriek and the others hopped further back, opening and closing their beaks. Bren moved further from the rail, towards the centre of the roof. Each crow he approached took to the air to reel away, adding to the black, flapping chaos that filled the air.

Featherly grimaced at his birds. Evie stared – with eyes wide and mouth still smothered – from beside the feathered throne. Catching her startled expression, Bren thought of the urn by his parents' bed. He thought of Mum and Dad, fretting and frightened, while his body froze to death just a street behind their own.

Again, fury and loathing filled his lungs. He turned his scowl to Featherly. "How *dare* you!" he shouted, his voice filling Furthermoor with its boom. "How dare you do this to me! How dare you do this to my mum and dad!"

Bren took an angry, quivering breath, barely noticing the chips of concrete falling around him.

"How *dare* you make me feel so small! How dare you make me feel so worthless!"

His bellow echoed around the roof, leaving sounds of cracking in its wake. Chunks of concrete began to fall from above, exposing the tree's bark and crystal leaves.

Grey stone smashed against the roof, scattering clouds of dust.

Bren's glare was still on Featherly. Featherly began to back away, his expression flitting between panic and scorn.

Bren wasn't done.

"And how dare you make me think it's all my fault – that I *deserve* everything hateful that's ever been done to me!"

Stalactites were falling now, smashing through pipes and taking down crows. Featherly cursed and stopped abruptly, standing his ground. His finger moved towards the watch.

"*That's mine!*" boomed Bren. Featherly's hands were forced to his ears, and the watch fell to his feet.

Bren kept striding and stooped to pick it up. When grey fingers swept to snatch it back, Bren raised a palm to Featherly's face. "Stay."

It took just a glance at the clock's mechanism to find the controls for the crows. A spin of a few cogs sent them circling around the tree – faster and faster, a black storm of feather and claw – until a flick at the watch hurled them into open air. A twitch of another cog made their wings jam up, so that they shrieked and plunged down the tower's height. Their cries grew quieter before ending with distant tinkles; the sound of birds smashing through emerald.

When Bren's eyes left the watch, Featherly was on his knees.

Bren took a step back, turning cogs as he went, until an almighty groaning and cracking was heard. Some of the tree's roots were tearing themselves from concrete.

Featherly didn't move – didn't even look up – while the roots crept tendril-like over pillars and vents to reach him. With a few tweaks of the watch, the roots rose around him, weaving themselves into a gnarly cage.

When the cage was finished, Bren closed his eyes and covered his face. He groaned with tiredness, with aching, then sat heavily by the cage and turned one more cog. A dry clacking came from the mumalike, and a warm hand was soon on Bren's back. It was Evie, crouching by his side.

"Bren," she breathed. "Are you okay?"

Bren released a hoarse breath. "I've never felt so… drained."

Evie nodded, rubbing his shoulder. "But you did it. You beat him. You stood up to yourself."

She shuffled to the cage to watch Featherly through the gaps between roots. Bren followed and saw Featherly flinching, with his face to one side. His thin hands rose to protect his head, and his wings looked smaller now. Frail and near-featherless.

"Lord of the land…" he whimpered.

Bren let the open watch sit in his palm. Featherly shivered and winced.

"Will you hurt me?" he rasped. "Will the young master…punish me?"

Bren was silent for some moments. Then he shook his head. "No. I'm not going to hurt you." He rubbed his tired eyes. "D'you know why?"

Featherly's shivering stopped. He lifted his head, just enough to swivel his eyes up to Bren.

Bren returned his gaze. "Because I'm better than that." He nodded slowly. "I'm better than you."

Featherly lowered his face, unable to look Bren in the eye.

"And you were wrong," continued Bren. "You've been wrong all along. I don't deserve what Shaun did to me. I don't deserve anything he's ever done to me. Okay?"

He huffed and rubbed his sore legs. "So maybe I'm shy. And yeah, I stay out of the way. I duck my head and I keep my mouth shut and I don't fight back. But so what? None of that means I deserve any of this. Not what you did, and not what Shaun's done."

Evie touched his shoulder. "Bren…"

Bren turned to her. "Yeah. I know." He got up and walked in a near-stagger to the railing. Evie took his hand to help him along.

As they reached the rail, Bren looked at Evie. "When I get back, things are going to change."

They were standing at the roof's brink. With a flick of

some cogs, a hole opened in the air beside the tower, a few metres below Bren's feet.

"I'll come back," said Bren, "when I'm out of that room and safe again."

Evie nodded.

Bren cast a glance back at Featherly. "Make sure you—"

"Just go already." And with that, Evie put both palms to Bren's back and shoved, hard enough to send him toppling over the rail.

A whoosh of windows and concrete, soaring past Bren as he plummeted. With the wind blasting his face, he fell through the hole and Furthermoor was gone.

Chapter Twenty-Six

Pulling the Pin

Hurtling through the ceiling, Bren hit the mattress with a thump. He curled up the moment he landed and – with his eyes squeezed shut – put the watch to his ear.

Seconds passed by.

Tock.

Tick.

Tock.

Tick.

Bren opened his eyes. He couldn't see much of anything, so he waited for them to adjust to the dim orange light. It came from the street light by the thinking room's window, which pocked the metal grating with ember-like specks.

Bren had never known such pain. His skin felt so cold it burned, and his addled senses made his stomach heave. Whenever he breathed in, the icy air seemed to sear his lungs.

It took a while for him to remember how to move his limbs. Groaning weakly, he sat up on the mattress, doing his best to stretch his cold, stiff arms.

Eventually Bren made it to his feet. They were so numb he felt like he was floating. He staggered a little, almost dropping back to the floor, then shuffled to the door. Thinking back to what had got him out in Furthermoor, he dropped to his knees and started breathing into the keyhole.

Bren tried the door but it wouldn't move. So he breathed into the keyhole again, this time for longer, trying his best to be patient. He heaved the handle once more, but nothing changed. No click nor clunk from the lock – no give at all.

This wasn't Featherly's Williamsborough. There was no trickery here. Just cold, hard truth: warming the keyhole wasn't going to work.

Bren went to his bag and pulled out his lunch box. He slammed it into the window but it crumpled against the glass, just as it had done in Furthermoor.

He was soon kicking the door with toes too numb to feel anything. He begged beneath his breath, but the door held as fast as ever.

Stepping back, Bren studied the door in the light from the grating. He refused to be beaten. He was leaving this room.

He glared at the door – at the grain of its wood, its metal handle, its door frame and brass hinges. He frowned at its handle and keyhole, and realized he'd been fixating on them. He needed to try something else. Lateral thinking.

His pupils moved up, left and down, following the door frame's course. When they met the door's upper hinge they stopped. Bren moved in for a closer look.

Most of the hinge's paint had flaked away, allowing Bren to see how it worked. It was a thin, vertical tube of metal made of smaller sections, some of which Bren realized were attached to the door's side, while the others were attached to the frame, keeping the door and frame together. And there was a metal nub, capping the tube's top.

Bren peered closer. Something must be holding the hinge together – something slotted through the metal tube's length, to keep its sections aligned.

Was that what the nub capping the tube was? The tip of whatever was holding the hinge together?

Bren turned away to look around the room. He needed something to attack that nub with. Some sort of tool.

He cursed beneath his breath. There was nothing.

No. Bren shook his head. He had his school backpack. There must be something in there. Something he could improvise with.

Crouching again by his bag, Bren tore off his remaining glove and opened his pencil case. After some rummaging, he took out a metal compass and studied its long, thin needle.

He returned to the door and started jabbing upwards at the bottom of the nub. A gasp left his lips when it rose a little, revealing the top of the pin that was slotted through the hinge's length.

Bren jabbed the nub again but it refused to move further, so he went to the window to grab his cracked lunch box. He used its undamaged side as a hammer, knocking the base of the compass while its needle pushed the nub. Bren saw the nub rising higher and higher, revealing more and more pin, until he was able to pull it out with his fingers.

As soon as the pin was gone, Bren saw the hinge sections loosen and separate – just by a couple of millimetres, but it was enough to tear a grunt of joy from his throat.

He was on his knees in an instant, knocking at the lower hinge until he could pull out its pin. Then – after throwing the compass and lunch box aside – he shook the door handle as hard as he could. The door's hinged side began to tilt out from the door frame, so Bren gripped it and pulled.

The door tipped backwards, twisting to one side as its bolt tore the frame. Bren leaped away to see it crash to the floor, then stepped across the wood and was out of the room.

He lurched along the landing, taking the corner and rushing down the stairs, before losing his footing and tumbling down the last steps. It took all his strength to drag himself up again – to push through the kitchen and into the garden.

After leaving the alley he hit Bradbury Avenue, heaving himself across the snow beneath the street lights. Moving his legs became harder and harder. They felt bone-cold and heavy, as if weighed down by sheaths of ice. The rush of energy he'd so recently ridden – that burst of adrenaline from conquering the door – had all but dribbled away. By the time Bren reached the Dale, he couldn't go on. It was Ballard Tower all over again.

He teetered on the corner, blinking drowsily at shops and dark, silent terraces. Staying upright was impossible, so he crumpled into the snow.

Home was just round the corner and down the next street. But it may as well have been a million light years away.

By now Bren was shivering uncontrollably. Every part of him was numb – so numb he couldn't feel the ground. But he could hear his breaths, rapid before but slowing now, leaving him in long, trembling wheezes.

He tried to think about Evie and his parents, praying the thought would help him, just as it had helped in the tower. But he couldn't focus on his thoughts, and realized with a dull stab of horror that he was struggling to visualize their faces. His brain felt as numb as his body.

Bren was hit by a sudden, overwhelming urge – as real and primal as it was strange and sickening – to take off his coat and burrow into the snow. But he couldn't move, so he used the last of his strength to open his mouth and cry out – to release a lonely, heartbroken sound into the street.

He stopped and had to close his eyes. His eyelids were too heavy.

And then he felt something. Fingers, lifting the back of his head. Bren heard a voice, seemingly from afar but close somehow too.

"Hey. Was that you? You okay?"

The voice rang a distant bell. Pressure on his hand. "Oh my god. You're *freezing*."

Bren knew that voice. It was the girl who usually sat outside the nail salon.

Her grip on his hand tightened and she called out for help, shattering the silence with a voice far stronger than Bren's.

Bren forced one of his eyes open. While the girl continued to shout, rectangles of light began to float in the darkness: windows, lit up here and there along the Dale. The more she hollered, the more lights appeared.

Bren's eyes closed again. He heard footsteps in the snow – more of them now. Someone else was shouting. Something about an ambulance.

"Bren?" Another voice. Panicked breaths. "*Bren?*"

A tear may have formed in Bren's eye; he was too numb to tell. But he knew that voice too.

Mum. It was Mum.

"Bren!" His head was released then cupped again, cradled on a lap. "Thank god we found you!" Mum's voice began to quiver. Her warm hands were in his hair. "What… what happened?"

Bren could just about move his lips. He pushed his breath between them, forming words in the icy air. "Shaun," he croaked. "Trapped me in…cold room. Door got jammed. Was all Shaun. Always been…Shaun…"

The ground seemed to rock. Something was being wrapped around him. He heard another voice.

"It's okay, son." Dad. "Just take it easy. Save your strength. You're safe now."

Bren wanted so badly to open his eyes – to see his parents' faces. But he couldn't.

New sounds. Heavy wheels crunching across slush. Blue pulses flashed against Bren's eyelids.

And then: darkness black as crows.

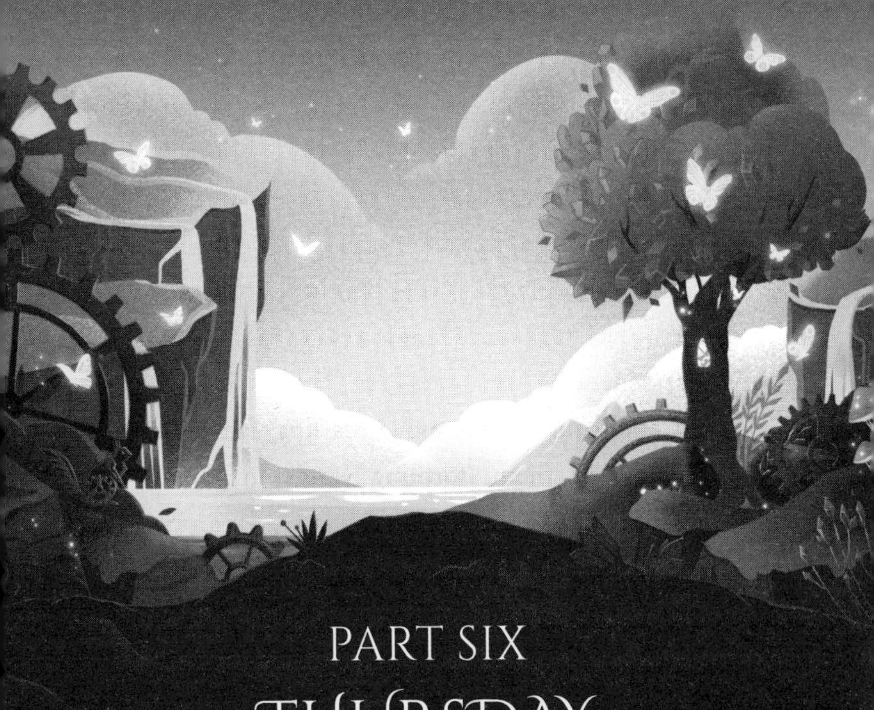

PART SIX
THURSDAY

Chapter Twenty-Seven

Curtains

When Bren opened his eyes, all went from black to blue and white. He rolled his pupils groggily left and right, confused by the chequered pattern all around him.

His dad's face came into focus, stubbly and pale.

"Bren?"

Something warm squeezed Bren's fingers. Someone's hand.

Another voice.

"Bren?" Mum's face appeared, shifting from a tired frown to a teary smile. "*Bren*, you're awake."

Bren could only mumble. He stared past his parents' haggard, relieved faces, trying to blink the blue and white into focus.

He finally realized what the chequered pattern was. It came from the curtain that surrounded all three of them, dangling from a rectangular rail on the ceiling. Sounds came from behind the thick fabric: soft voices, muted footsteps.

Bren's eyes moved down and across, taking in the white bed with its raised rails; the plastic chair behind each parent, one at each side of the bed; the wire dangling from the plastic clip on his finger.

He swallowed drily, trying his tongue.

"Is this...hospital?"

Mum put her hand on the side of his head. "Yes. You're in hospital. But don't worry, you'll be out soon enough. They just want to keep an eye on you. For a little longer."

"Eye on me?"

Dad took his hand. His hair was a greying shambles. "You had hypothermia, son. From the cold." The skin around his eyes wrinkled. He gave a weak smile. "Luckily we found you just in time. Or at least...Beth found you." Those creases deepened. "I dread to think—"

"Not now," interrupted Mum, tapping Dad's hand.

Bren shifted against the pillow, trying to raise himself. He could remember it now. Lying in the snow on the Dale.

"I was trapped." Bren's drowsy gaze moved back and forth between Mum and Dad. "In the house on Bradbury Avenue. It was...Shaun."

Mum's expression darkened. "We know what happened. Shaun confessed. To all of it."

"Confessed?"

"He's just outside," murmured Dad. "Been waiting there for—"

Mum cleared her throat, stopping him with a terse shake of her head.

"Shaun's here?" asked Bren.

Mum's lips stiffened, causing freckles to gather around her mouth. "With his dad. They've been asking to see you. But we didn't let them. I'm sure Shaun's the last person you want to see right now."

Bren stared at the curtain, listening to the clip-clop of soles against the rubbery floor. Seconds passed before he spoke. "Can you let him in?"

"What?"

"I want to see him."

Mum just stared. Dad frowned, scratching his nose. "You sure you want to do that, matey? After what he did?"

Bren nodded and raised himself further, so that his back was against the pillow. "Just a few minutes. If that's okay?"

Mum continued to stare while Dad shuffled towards the curtain. "I guess –" he began – "if that's what you really want? I'll see if they're still around."

As Dad left, Mum came close to put a palm on Bren's cheek. "You sure you want to see him, Bren?"

Bren managed a smile. "Sure I'm sure."

Mum was studying him closely. "Okay. It's your call."

She nodded to herself with an eye on the curtain, then looked at him again. "And Bren?"

"Yeah?"

"I'm not upset that you didn't tell us. About the things Shaun was doing at school. I realize it can't have been… easy for you. But…" She bit her lower lip, sad now. "You would tell us now, wouldn't you? If anyone was ever mean to you again?"

Bren met her gaze, then nodded sincerely.

"Don't be scared to make a fuss, Bren. It's never a fuss. We can help you. We'll always help you. Okay?"

Bren swallowed drily. "I'm sorry I didn't tell you. It's just… I didn't want to… I mean…" His voice began to thicken. "You and Dad had so much to deal with after… after…"

He struggled to go on. Tears were brimming in Mum's eyes. With her lips clamped and trembling, she took his hand in both of her own and squeezed it tight. "Evie," she croaked. "I know. Evie."

She hugged Bren then. He could feel her tears, wet and warm against his cheek.

Mum pulled away, took his hand once more. "Bren. I'm the one who should say sorry. I know I've not been around much. I've kept myself busy. *Too* busy. It's been a way to…to cope, I guess. To distract myself. From what happened." She sniffed, brushing away some red hair stuck to her cheek.

Bren stroked her palm with his thumb. "I've been the same, Mum. I've not spent time with you when you're home. Dad neither. I don't really spend time with…anyone."

"You're like your dad," said Mum. "He never leaves the house. If you didn't have to go to school, I bet you wouldn't either. We never go anywhere. It's like we're all…hiding. Not just from the world – from each other." She sniffed again, sighing. "It's hardly what Evie would have wanted, is it?"

Bren spoke around the lump in his throat. "No. It's not."

Mum watched him for some moments before nodding to herself. "So let's stop hiding. Let's team up." A smile touched her lips. "Like we used to, when Evie was around."

Bren gave a weak smile. "I'd like that."

Footsteps beyond the screen. Dad parted the curtain and peered at them both. "Bren? They're here. You sure about this?"

Bren nodded. Dad let Shaun and his dad through, before coming in himself and closing the curtain.

While Shaun stayed by the foot of the bed and kept his face low, his dad stood beside him with his legs parted and arms crossed. His expression was grim – sour and defiant – beneath his combed-back hair.

A terse silence began to build, until Shaun's dad tapped his son's arm with the back of his hand. "Well say it then! We didn't come all this way so you could mope about."

Shaun raised his eyes briefly to Bren, then looked moodily at the floor.

"Sorry," he mumbled. "Was an accident. Didn't know the door was gonna jam..." He shuffled from one foot to the other.

Before Shaun could say more, Bren took a deep breath of the ward's sterile air. "Shaun," he began. "Look at me."

Shaun's face lifted again, sulky and sullen.

Bren shook his head with his eyes set on Shaun's. "Even if that door hadn't jammed, Shaun... Even if it hadn't, you still dragged me from the street and forced me into that room. You still locked me in and made me say all those... those *horrible* things. You still laughed with your mates on the other side of the door."

Bren felt his fingers curling, clenching into fists.

"And even if you hadn't done all that, you still pushed me around in school. You still shoved me into lockers and walls. You still called me names and punched me whenever you felt like punching someone. You still made me eat dirt and call myself awful things, and you laughed through the lot of it like it was the funniest thing in the world. So don't you *dare* try to make this about that lock."

Shaun's entire body tightened. His lips thinned and a pink glow – perhaps anger, perhaps shame – flushed the paleness from his cheeks.

Bren eyed him for a moment, before speaking again.

"I'm done with it, okay? I've had enough. I'm not going to be anyone's victim. Not any more. I'm sick of it. I'm sick of people looking the other way. Of taking punches for everyone else."

He felt someone squeeze his hand. It was Mum. She wore the steadfast, steely expression she'd passed on to Evie, but Bren could see tears in her eyes again. He glanced over to Dad, who was looking uncomfortably at his fidgeting hands.

Shaun's dad gave a huff. He shoved his son's shoulder before addressing Bren's parents.

"Shaun's not the sharpest tool in the box. He's not got the best handle on his temper. And it looks like he's been taking stuff out on your boy. It's pathetic, I know." He shook his head in disgust.

Shaun's face turned even redder. Bren noticed that the hardness had left his eyes; they looked softer now. Hurt, even.

Shaun's dad tutted at his son. "Honest, Shaun. You need to get a grip. It's embarrassing. This stuff you've been doing to this boy…" He shook his head again. "The police are involved and everything."

Shaun muttered at the floor, "Wouldn't be the first time they've been round."

"You what?" Shaun's dad bristled. He stepped up to Shaun, jutting his chin towards his face. "What did you say? You fancy saying it again? Cos if you do I'll—"

"*Stop it.*" The words shot from Bren's mouth; there was no holding them back. "Just leave him alone, yeah? You're as bad as he is! In fact...you're *worse.*" He clutched the bed sheets, almost shaking with anger. "I've seen the way you are with Shaun, always putting him down, pushing him around. No wonder he's the way he is!"

Shaun's dad's eyes were wide with fury. He aimed them straight at Bren, stepping towards the bed and gripping its end. "You'd better watch your mouth and mind your own business. You think you've got a right to—"

He stopped when Dad came close, barging gently so that Shaun's dad was forced to let go of the bed.

Bren's dad couldn't look at Shaun's. His eyes were fixed awkwardly on the curtain. But his words were firm. "I think you'd better leave."

Shaun's dad hesitated. His eyes darted from Dad to Mum – who'd taken a step towards him, though her hand still held Bren's – and then to the nurse who'd just parted the curtain.

"What's all this commotion?" asked the nurse. "This is a hospital ward. People are trying to rest."

Mum scowled at Shaun's dad. "Just go. Get out."

Shaun's dad scowled back while pushing past the nurse, then sneered at Bren, "Look at you. You're a runt and a grass. I bet you had it all coming – everything Shaun did to you."

Bren gazed coolly back at him. "No," he said, calmly, matter-of-factly. "I didn't."

Shaun's dad was soon gone, stomping across the ward and barking his son's name. Shaun turned to follow through the curtain, but threw a confused glance at Bren before following his dad.

When they'd both left, Bren sank back down into the bed. His parents took their seats on either side of him.

"You okay?" asked Dad. Mum was holding Dad's hand now, with her arm across the bed.

Bren nodded tiredly. The rush of adrenaline was dying away, leaving him spent and weary. But he was glowing in his sleepiness. He'd just stood up not only to Shaun, but to Shaun's dad as well. It felt dreamlike. It felt good.

He glanced at the hospital tag on his wrist. "Where's Evie's watch?"

"At home," said Mum. "In your room."

Bren nodded, closing his eyes.

"Do you need it?"

Bren gave this some thought before shaking his head. He sank deeper into bed. "No. Not right now."

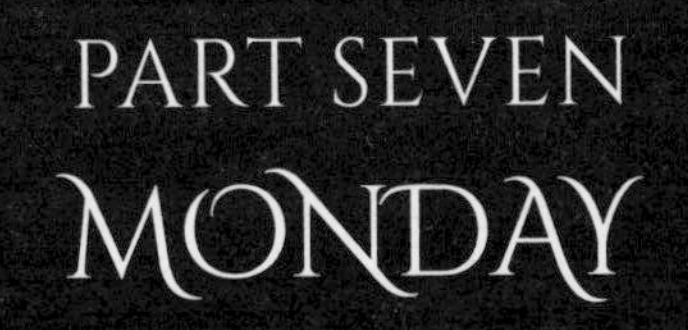

PART SEVEN
MONDAY

Chapter Twenty-Eight
Somewhere Beautiful

With a circle still in the sky above him, Bren dropped from a branch and strolled towards Evie. She was in the clearing by Ballard Tower, lounging on her back on a picnic blanket.

He nudged her with the toe of his school shoe.

"Hey, big sis."

"Hey, little bro."

Bren's gaze travelled up the tower. He could see the roots of the tunnel tree – now entirely free of concrete – gripping its edges. Leaves of emerald glittered in the sky.

The frost was gone from the forest, and Bren had cleared the meadow of Featherly's streets; they'd reminded him too much of the mumalike and dadalike. But he hadn't been able to bring himself to remove the tower. Whenever he looked at its summit he was reminded of how far he'd come.

He pointed towards the tunnel tree. "How's Featherly?"

Evie's eyes followed his finger. "Last time I checked he wasn't up there."

"What?"

"The cage is empty."

"He's escaped?"

Evie shrugged, unbothered. "Nah. I think he's gone."

"Gone?"

"Yeah. Just like that."

"Just like that?"

Evie rolled her eyes. "Are you going to repeat everything I say?"

Bren smirked. "Are you going to repeat everything I say?"

"Grow up."

Bren chuckled and took a seat on the blanket. He checked the woods again, then nodded slowly to himself. "He's gone."

The siblings sat in silence, listening to clockwork chirps and birdsong. Bren rubbed his nose and shifted a little. "Sorry, by the way."

"For what?"

"Not visiting since Friday."

Still smiling, Evie pulled herself up. She sat facing Bren with her calves crossed. "That's alright. It's good."

"It is?" Bren fidgeted with his fingers. "I feel sort of bad about it. Not being around over the weekend. I should have come to keep you company. But I...I've been..."

"With Mum and Dad?"

"Well, yeah." Bren hugged his knees, rocking on the blanket.

Evie put a hand on his leg to stop him squirming. "Hey. It's okay. I'm glad you guys are hanging out." She grinned. "My ears have been burning. Have you been talking about me?"

Bren nodded, smiling a little too. "Yeah. We have." His smile slipped. "But that's no excuse to spend less time here."

"I'd say it's the perfect excuse." Evie arched her neck, gazing peacefully across concrete and crystal. "I was thinking of leaving anyway."

Bren's eyebrows rose. "Leaving?"

Evie nodded, before flicking some hair from the shoulder of her summer dress.

"But where would you go? How would that even… work?"

Evie shrugged. "No idea. But I feel like a change."

"Where will you go?"

"Somewhere beautiful."

"Beautiful…" echoed Bren. He was still trying to grasp what Evie was saying.

He blinked hard, his throat suddenly swollen. "Hang on. You can't just go. I'll…I'll miss you."

"I'll miss you too, little bro. But I won't *really* be gone.

You know that. I mean, sure, I may not be here..." She touched Bren's forehead with her finger. "Not like I am now. But I'll always be here, right?" She tapped Bren's chest.

She was harder to see now, blurring in Bren's welling eyes.

"Right?" repeated Evie, still smiling.

Bren swallowed, forced a hoarse reply. "Right."

Evie got up and offered her hand. She eyed his school jumper. "Lunch break, is it?"

"Yeah."

After taking a long look around Furthermoor, Bren wiped his eyes, took Evie's hand and let her pull him up.

He sniffed, clearing his throat. "I'll see you...around, then?"

"I'll always be around, Bren. One way or another." And with that, Evie took her brother in her arms.

Bren hugged her back, pushing his damp eyes into her shoulder. He felt her hand in his hair.

"Go," she said.

With a nod, Bren pulled away, adjusted the watch and made for a revolving tree. When he'd climbed through the crystal canopy, he looked down towards the clearing and saw Evie by the blanket. She was waving happily at him, with the green frames of her glasses flashing in sunlight.

Bren waved back, and kept waving until Evie made shooing motions with her hands.

After one last wave at his sister, Bren started climbing again, then hauled himself up through the hole in the sky.

Tock.

Tick.

Tock.

Tick.

After the drum kit had reassembled itself, Bren lingered with Evie's watch in his palm. The tears from Furthermoor had followed him into the music room, and he wiped them away while gazing at the drums.

A vibration in his pocket. Bren took out his phone. It was a text from Mum.

How about camping this weekend? We could go to the Peaks. Lots of memories there. We'll make new ones too. You can show us the tree Evie used to talk about.

Bren smiled while texting his reply.

Sounds great.

After closing his eyes and taking some slow breaths, Bren pocketed the watch, left the arts block and started along the path. The air was still chilly, but the snow had all melted. The sun was doing its best to burn through dull clouds.

A chattering from the trees. Bren froze.

"Great..." he mumbled, looking up at two crows who

were eyeing him from a nearby branch. Though every nerve told him to pull up his coat's hood and flee, he stayed put, clenching his lips and eyeing the crows, just as he'd done on Ballard Tower.

One of the birds cocked its head. The other let out an ugly caw.

With his heart pounding – with every hair rising on the nape of his neck – Bren maintained his dogged gaze and took a step forward.

As soon he did, the crows dived for him.

Bren yelped, flapping his hands to beat the birds away. But the more he flailed, the more they clawed. He felt a nip draw blood from his hand, and was about to shout for help when something large flew into his vision, knocking a crow away. As he staggered backwards, he saw someone swipe at the birds with a backpack, sending them squawking into the sky.

Bren's chin dropped when he realized who it was.

Shaun watched the crows go and put his backpack over his shoulder. He turned his frosty gaze to Bren.

"You alright?"

Bren was panting on the path. He pushed his palm against his chest, willing his heart rate to slow. "Yeah," he gasped, staring at Shaun. "Um… Thank…you?"

Shaun didn't say anything. Instead he just stood there, looking Bren up and down.

Bren began to feel uncomfortable, but he didn't move or break his gaze. After some time had passed, Shaun gave a silent, respectful nod, then turned and walked away.

As he watched Shaun go, Bren heard someone running up behind him. He turned to see Cary skidding to a stop.

"Bren!" puffed Cary. "I saw Shaun! Was he giving you hassle?"

A shrug and shake of the head. "Nah. He's stopped that stuff now."

"You think?"

"Yeah. I do." Bren began to smile. It was good to see Cary again. "Hey, did you get your phone back?"

Cary squinted awkwardly, rubbing the back of his neck. "Um...yeah. I did. But listen, I'm really sorry about what happened after I told my parents. I wish I'd talked to you first – you know, figured out how to handle this stuff together." He frowned at the ground. "I thought Shaun would drop it after the school got involved. That's worked before. With other bullies, I mean." His eyes lifted. "If I'd known what Shaun would do..."

"You heard what happened?"

"Yeah. On Bradbury Avenue. The whole school's been talking about it." Cary slapped Bren's elbow, trying to smile but not quite managing it. "I'm really glad you got out of that room, bud. If you hadn't..."

"Hey." Bren tapped Cary's arm in return, trying to

reassure him. "Chill, Cary. I got out. And in some ways… it's thanks to you."

Cary looked confused. "It was me telling the school that got you trapped in there."

"No, Cary. *Shaun* got me trapped in there. You just did what you thought was best. You were trying to help. Don't blame yourself."

Cary squinted at Bren, then sighed with a shrug. "I just thought I could handle Shaun. I thought I'd figured him out. But it just goes to show, right? Bullies aren't one-size-fits-all."

"Guess not."

Cary cleared his throat, looking sheepish again. "Same goes for the people they pick on. Like…I heard, you know? From some of the other pupils."

"Heard what?"

"About your sister."

Bren's lips parted, but he didn't know what to say. It was his turn to lower his eyes.

"I mean," continued Cary, "I knew you were sad about something. But if I'd had any idea you were going through…something like that…" He shuffled his feet. "It probably wasn't fair of me – to expect you to be brave or chummy or whatever. I know I wouldn't be."

Bren's thoughts went back to Evie. He remembered something she'd said in Furthermoor, then looked up to flash Cary a genuine smile. "I bet you would. Just not like you think. Bravery isn't always loud. It can be quiet too."

Cary didn't look like he understood, but that was fine with Bren.

Bren shrugged and laughed, trying to clear the air. "Hey, do you fancy a kickabout before the bell rings?"

"Um…sure? You wanna go somewhere quiet?"

"Nah. There's a big game in the playground, isn't there?"

Cary's eyebrows rose. "You want to join the match?"

"Sure I do."

"Oh. Okay." Cary nodded to himself. That cocky smile was returning to his face. "I mean, sure. Just make sure we're on the same team, yeah? I saw your skills in the garden."

The pair of them were soon heading down the path and hitting the playground. After dumping their backpacks, they sprinted onto the makeshift pitch. Bren thought he heard some cheers. Cary whooped and cackled and called to the players, and Bren laughed too, ready for the ball that was soaring his way.

THE END

If you have been affected by some of the issues raised in this book, the following organisations can help or provide info:

Kidscape provides advice and support with bullying including free ZAP workshops for children and families impacted by a bullying situation, the Parent Advice Line and teacher training.
www.kidscape.org.uk

The Anti-Bullying Alliance are a unique coalition of organisations and individuals, working together to achieve their vision to stop bullying and create safer environments in which children and young people can live, grow, play and learn. They are part of the National Children's Bureau. They are united against bullying.
www.anti-bullyingalliance.org.uk

Child Bereavement UK helps children and young people (up to age 25), parents, and families, to rebuild their lives when a child grieves or when a child dies. They also provide training to professionals, equipping them to provide the best possible care to bereaved families.
Helpline: 0800 02 888 40
support@childbereavementuk.org
www.childbereavementuk.org

AUTHOR'S NOTE

SPOILER ALERT

Imagination is so much more than daydreams and fluff. It's a force, as vital to our lives as the blood in our veins.

Imagination is behind the best and worst in humanity. The wheel only exists because someone imagined it. The same goes for democracy, medicine, charity, and all that's good. But by the same token, everything man-made that hurts, represses and harms also exists because of imagination.

So does the book you're holding in your hands.

Furthermoor began as an author's whim. I fell in love with the idea of a jewelled mechanical forest, and wanted to use it as a setting. But I wasn't sure how to do so without writing a fantasy novel. I've always preferred dodging pigeonholes to falling squarely into them, and wanted to use a fantastical setting without writing a fantasy book. But how?

The answer came to me – as it so often does – while I was doing the dishes: I could set the story not only in contemporary urban life, but also in the protagonist's imagination. In imagination, anything is possible. A jewelled forest can exist not because of magic, but because someone thinks it up. Imagination is where fantasy actually *exists*.

Another thought occurred to me. What if – as well as using both urban and imagined settings – I found a way to blend the two? I visualised a modern town consumed by crystal foliage, and started scrubbing very excitedly at those dishes. I was on to something.

I researched imagined worlds, and soon came across a psychiatric condition called maladaptive daydreaming. People who suffer from this become so absorbed in their rich, detailed, imaginary worlds – knowing all the while that they're not real – that it has a negative impact on their lives. They shun their real family and friends in favour of imagined companions, sidekicks, siblings. They get so consumed by their imaginary exploits that their real-life relationships and careers suffer. It's an addiction; a preference for fantasy worlds over reality – something I found all too easy to relate to, particularly as an author.

I was fascinated by this notion, and decided to write a novel in which a protagonist – a little like those maladaptive daydreamers – becomes trapped in his imaginary sanctuary, in a way that puts him in danger in the physical world. It felt like an intriguing way to explore not only reality versus fantasy, but also the blurred lines between the two, and how each impacts the other.

Imagination isn't *Furthermoor*'s only theme, of course. This is also a novel about bullying.

It's so sad that, when I pondered what might cause a young person to create an imaginary sanctuary, bullying came immediately to mind. It just goes to show how pervasive bullying is.

I'm very lucky in that, beyond the occasional tease as a loner in school – yes, Cary's backstory draws a little from my own – I was never prey to extended bouts of bullying. But I've witnessed it, not only in school, but also in college, in the workplace, on social media, in the streets. I daresay we all have.

I'm not brave at all. I'm a coward, in fact, and I dread confrontation. I try not to turn a blind eye, though, and in many cases have refused to do so. I've asked schoolmates to ease off on name calling, and one time climbed through a toilet window to help someone who'd been locked into a cubicle "for laughs". But in hindsight, I can also think of situations where I wish I'd done more. We learn every day.

I think about bullying and power a lot, and often wonder why, in all walks of life, people bully. So it was interesting to spend lots of time researching bullying for this book – to get into the heads of those giving it out and those at the receiving end. As I read real-life stories and made notes on professional advice, it quickly became obvious that my novel could never give clear, definitive guidance on bullying. These situations are too complex and so full of hurt, often for many parties involved. So I hope that *Furthermoor* at least encourages an appreciation of this complexity, and of the care required when handling these scenarios, while putting across a few things I feel *do* apply in every case.

Anyone being bullied shouldn't suffer in silence. They don't deserve to be bullied, and they shouldn't feel ashamed. And anyone witnessing bullying should do their best to make it stop, but in a way that's safe for everyone involved.

All much easier said than done, of course.

That's why *Furthermoor* is dedicated to the wallflowers – I speak as someone who's attracted bullies simply by being shy – and to those who refuse to look the other way. If you've ever helped anyone suffering at the hands of bullies in their many, many forms, thank you. You make the world a kinder, fairer place. And if you're being bullied yourself, don't be ashamed and don't take the blame, and please look into the help offered by the organisations on page 275. You're braver than you think.

ACKNOWLEDGEMENTS

I'd like to thank the following folk for being so super. They've all done their bit to keep me going and make this book happen.

Wanda, my wife and friend, and frankly an astonishing human being.

Oskar and Charlie, my pride and my joy. Extra thanks to Oskar for being a *Furthermoor* guinea pig, and to Charlie for his clownery and cuddles.

My wonderful mum and dad, Sue and Graham, and my siblings, Elvis, Kelly and Graham. Also sending hugs to my wider and extended family.

Laura Susijn, my agent, for believing in me from the beginning.

Stephanie King, my superlative editor, for chiselling my story-lumps into the best books they can be (and for being so gracious whenever pointing out that I've gone too far).

Sarah Stewart for being there, third time round, with her editing smarts.

Maisie Chan for her sensitivity read and incredibly helpful input, and Eva Man for her thoughtful suggestions.

Tilda Johnson for the return of her eagle eye, and Alice Moloney and Gareth Collinson for their proofreading powers. Thanks also to Alice for thinking up such excellent discussion questions for this book.

Anna Kuptsova for her perfect cover illustration, Will Steele for his ever-brill design work, and Penelope Mazza for her spine-tingling animations.

Sarah Cronin for typesetting and text design, and for making this book as gorgeous inside as out.

Jessica Feichtlbauer, Kat Jovanovic and Hannah Reardon Steward of Usborne's marketing team, for their brilliance, time and generosity.

Samuel J. Halpin, A.M. Howell and Serena Patel. I truly believe, dearest Class of '18, that, together, if we turn our eyes from the stars and hang like bats from our door frames, we can be more Dan.

All those awesome Independent Usborne Partners, with shout-outs to Dionne Lakey (superstar!), Sarah Sumner (all the best, Sarah!) and Katy Wedderburn [insert Jeff Goldblum gif here].

All at Usborne HQ, for creating such superb and

inspiring books, and for giving my stories a home among them.

I'd also like to thank all the individuals and organisations who get books into the hands of young readers, and who nurture the passion for reading that serves us so well throughout our lives. A few folk – admittedly largely from the top of my head – include Jess Alex, Jasbinder Bilan, the Book Whisperer, Alison Brumwell, CILIP, Jo Clarke, Christopher Edge, Eksmo, Jonathan Emmett, Empathy Lab, Kitty Empire, Scott Evans, Jane Etheridge, Lily Fae, FCBG, Sarah Forestwood, Nikki Gamble, Lucy Georgeson, Ben Harris, Gavin Hetherington, Inspire Libraries, Just Imagine, Katrina Reads, lovereading4kids.co.uk, Tracy Lowe, George Napthine, Megan Nicholson, Fiona Noble, Oxford University Press, PiXL, Kate Poels, the Reading Realm, Read It Daddy, Imogen Russell Williams, *The School Librarian*, schoolreadinglist.co.uk, Scope for Imagination, Simon Smith, Chris Soul, Jacqui Sydney, Timaş, Samantha Thomas, Carol Williams, Alex Wheatle, World Book Day and VIP Reading. There are many, many more people spreading book-joy, and who by extension spread literacy, empathy, critical thinking and good mental health. To all the book champions not listed here, forgive me, and thank you for your amazing, crucial work.

Closer to home, I'd like to thank the following lovely peeps.

My brothers from other mothers: Jason Holt, Neil Marsden and Gavin Macfarlane.

Those beautiful Bees: Jim Alexander, Phil Formby, Kirsty Fox and Dan Layton.

The Savoy Grand gang: Chris Baldwin, Christophe Dejous, Neil Johnson, Graham Langley, Kieran O'Riordan and Mark Spivey.

Those pleated lemons and MMPC legends: Richard Dytch and Matt Eris.

Sandeep Mahal, Leanne Moden, Matt Turpin and all at Nottingham City of Literature.

Charlotte Malik, Emily Landsborough, Lynne Towle, Julia Paynton, Marykate McGrath and the rest of the team at the Literacy Trust. It's been such a privilege to work with you.

Ross Bradshaw, Pippa Hennessy and co of the Five Leaves Bookshop – and all the other indie booksellers too!

I'd also like to thank all the children and teens I've met during author visits and events. They leave me feeling hopeful and inspired, every single time.

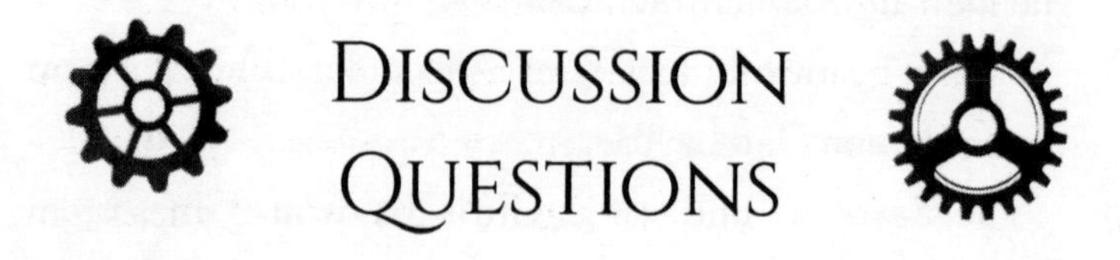

Discussion Questions

1. Think about the world of *Furthermoor* with its cogs and mechanisms. Why do you think Bren imagined it this way? Why do you think he created it in the first place?

2. What were your initial impressions of Cary? What did you think about the way he dealt with Shaun's bullying?

3. Mr Okorafor's English assigment for Bren is to write about how the following quote relates to *Animal Farm*: "Power tends to corrupt and absolute power corrupts absolutely." How might this quote also relate to *Furthermoor*?

4. "The uncanny" is a term used to describe things that are unsettling because they are familiar, but strange –

like seeing a picture of yourself, only your eyes are the wrong colour and that makes it a bit scary. Can you think of ways that Darren Simpson has used this idea of "familiar but not quite" to create unease in *Furthermoor*?

5. Look at the different ways Mum, Dad and Bren are all dealing with the loss of Evie. How did you feel when you discovered Evie had died?

6. Bren and Evie think up the world of Furthermoor when they are on holiday, camping in a beautiful forest. If you could create an imaginary world to visit one day, what would it be like? Would you base it on somewhere you've been, or come up with something entirely new?

7. Bren urges Cary not to tell anyone about Shaun's bullying. Why do you think he does this? Do you think Cary did the right thing by telling his parents?

8. Think about the different parents we meet and hear about in *Furthermoor* – Bren's, Shaun's and Cary's. How do their actions impact their children? Did meeting these characters' families affect the way you thought about them?

9. Look at the cover of *Furthermoor*, illustrated by Anna Kuptsova. How has she shown the two different sides of Furthermoor we experience in the story?

10. On page 120, Cary tells Bren that he thinks Shaun is a wimp because "Bullies always are." Do you agree with this statement? Why do you think Shaun bullies Bren?

11. Look at Chapter Nineteen, from page 183 to 191. How does the author, Darren Simpson, build tension, as Bren starts to realise something is wrong in his world?

12. Evie says that "Bravery isn't always big and loud, Bren. It can be quiet too." Do you agree with this? What do you think is the bravest thing any character does in *Furthermoor*? Is it big and loud, or more quiet? Think about the world you live in, and make a list of brave things that are big and loud, and a list of brave things that are quieter.

13. Lots of characters in *Furthermoor* "turn a blind eye", which means they pretend not to notice something's wrong. Why might someone do this? Is it because they don't want to fix the problem, or because they don't know how? Are you ever tempted to turn a blind eye to things? Do you think it helps?

14. Do you think Featherly is a villain in this story? Were you surprised when Featherly's identity was revealed?

15. Think about how the story ends for characters like Bren, Evie, Cary and Shaun. Do you think *Furthermoor* has a happy ending?

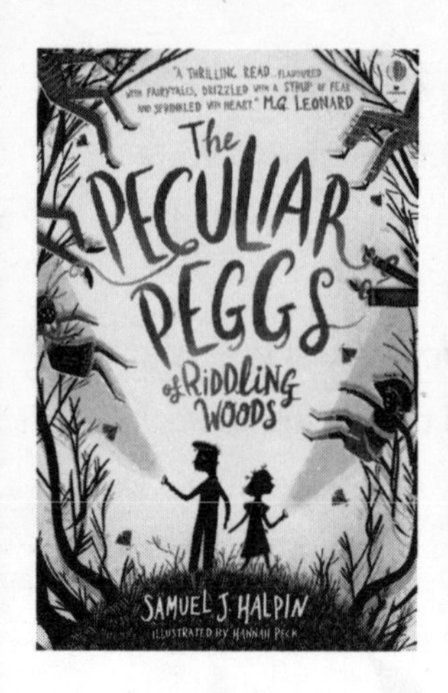

Love this book? Love Usborne fiction

Join us online for the all latest news on Usborne fiction, plus extracts, interviews and reviews

usborne.com/Fiction

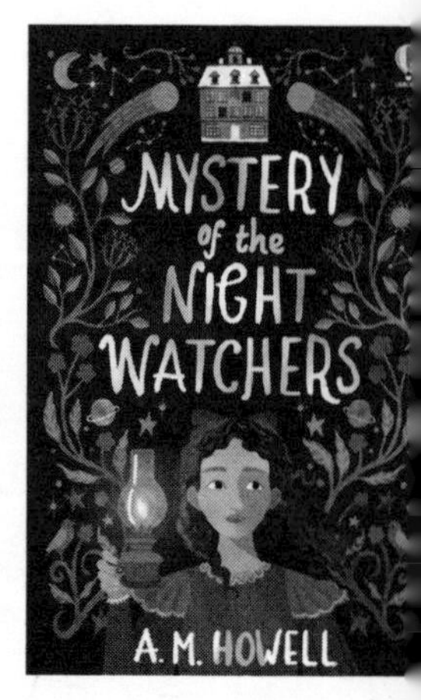